First paperback edition August 2024

Book cover design by getcovers.com

ISBN 978-1-7779003-5-9 (paperback)

ISBN 978-1-7779003-4-2 (eBook)

ISBN 978-1-7779003-6-6 (hardcover)

https://winnzwordz.com

CONTENTS

~

This book is dedicated to my mother, Amma.

Dearest Amma,

There was once a budding author

Who thought her books didn't matter

Amma said, "Keep writing..."

Amma said, "Don't stop publishing..."

"Your stories will find their way to your readers.

Especially, to my darling granddaughter."

~

Chapter 1

Rory

I shifted my weight from one foot to another as I waited in line to drop my luggage at Strollfield International Airport. It had been over thirty minutes, and the counter was still far away. I sighed as I fiddled with the pull-up trolley handle of my suitcase. I would have to wait at least another forty-five more minutes before my turn.

The person behind me let out a rather loud chuckle, and I turned.

Sorry, he mouthed, pointing to his phone.

I gave him a thumbs-up. "All good."

He adjusted his headphones and continued to be engrossed in whatever he was watching. I tried to peek at his device but stopped myself.

I wasn't allowed to do this. If I couldn't stay away from cell phones for a few minutes, how was I supposed to do so for two whole weeks?

"Rory Matthews, remember what the Mobile Rehab website said," I told myself in a low tone. "No cell phones. No tablets. And no screens. It's just for two weeks. You can do this."

"The Mobile Rehab" was a two-week program in Hong Kong where cell phone addicts like me were forced to stay without any digital devices or screens. The founders of the program, Mr. and Mrs. Hong, former addicts themselves, felt that staying away from smartphones and focusing on nondigital activities would decrease our dependency on them, thereby helping us overcome our addiction.

I hoped this would work, because lately, I could not stay away from my cell phone at all. If it was not with me, I felt as if a part of my body was missing. And I knew this was unhealthy.

Like right now. Everyone in the airport, young and old, were on their phones. Some of them were so absorbed by their devices, they wouldn't move forward in the line until a ground staff member requested they close the gap. And instead of feeling proud that I was not one of the distracted passengers, I envied them and pictured snatching one of their devices and watching short videos until my eyes hurt.

Before I let my imagination get the better of me, I decided to get some coffee. I informed the person behind me I would be right back. He nodded and gave me a thumbs-up sign.

Within ten minutes, I'd bought my coffee from a vending machine nearby and resumed my place in the line. I sipped my beverage and decided to listen to some music. This was going to be more difficult than I thought.

I placed my coffee cup on the floor next to my suitcase and removed my backpack from my shoulder. I opened it and fished out a silver-colored device. I checked the battery compartment and confirmed it was loaded correctly. I wiped some nonexistent dust off its surface, thankful that this old thing could keep me company today. According to Mrs. Hong, it was not okay to bring any digital music, but this was acceptable.

"Mommy, look. What's that thing he's got?" a child ask loudly. "It looks weird."

I felt self-conscious as everyone in the airport looked at me. A few people pointed their phones at me and started filming.

"Guys, you won't believe what I'm seeing right now," a man said, placing his phone closer to my hands. "It's a Walkman with an actual cassette tape inside it." He tapped me on my shoulder. "Sir, do you mind if I show this to my followers?"

I mutely shook my head as he continued.

"I used to listen to these when I was a teenager. Seeing this makes me feel so old. I'm getting nostalgic. Those were simpler times, when we didn't have cell phones or tablets or social media." He turned his phone toward me. "You look young. How did you get your hands on a Walkman?"

"My parents gave it to me," I answered sheepishly, hoping he wouldn't prod me further. I didn't want to be interviewed right now.

"Sir, ma'am, videography is prohibited in the airport," a ground staff member informed the vlogger and the other people who were recording me. "Please get back in line."

I heaved a sigh of relief as people lowered their phones reluctantly, though they continued to look in my direction. I tried not to acknowledge them and sipped on my coffee as I plugged my earphones. I pressed "play" on my Walkman and almost spit out my coffee when I heard the "music" that was playing.

"Our digestive system starts with our mouth and ends with our anus. When we eat, our teeth and our saliva cut down the food particles into smaller pieces. Saliva that is secreted from salivary glands contains salivary amylase..."

This was my sister, Riley's voice. She had the habit of recording her notes so that she could listen to them later. Couldn't she have mentioned that somewhere on the cassette cover? Or did she play a prank on me? It was probably the latter, knowing her.

Now, thanks to her, I was stuck with a boring anatomy lesson as entertainment for the entire flight.

I stopped the Walkman and unplugged my earphones, but people were still staring at me.

The vlogger looked at me curiously and mouthed, *what happened?*

The last thing I wanted was for him and his followers to laugh at my expense about my situation. So, I plugged my earphones back in and pretended to groove to the "music," pleading with the universe to make the line move faster.

After what seemed like hours, I finally dropped my luggage at the counter, completed the security check, and waited at the gate for boarding. Not wanting to attract any more attention, I removed a book from my backpack, though I don't like to read. I prefer audio-books any day.

My avid reader friends, Tina Lauren and Aiden Wilkins had given me books for this trip. Aiden writes YA contemporary fiction under the pseudonym Enida W. Alexander, and Tina's dad, Walt Lauren, is a bestselling psychological thriller author.

I'd started reading the thriller when I heard two voices talking about me.

"First a Walkman, now a book. This young man is taking us back in time."

"I know, right? And he's wearing an analog watch in this day and age. It's refreshing to see youngsters not glued to their phones, though. I wish my daughter learned something from him. She's on her phone or tablet all the time. I have to disconnect our Wi-Fi to make her put her devices down."

"My son refuses to play outside or go camping with us because he finds them boring. All he wants to do is to play online games."

"Technology is really ruining our kids."

"Anyway, have you seen this new reel? It's hilarious."

"Of course I have. I've seen all of them by that creator. These short videos are so addictive."

I shook my head and chuckled to myself. How ironic. Who was the addict there? The parents or their children?

I could relate to this situation. Both my parents were doctors, and my older sister was in medical school. When Mom and Dad come home after a long day, they were tired. Their method of unwinding was to watch television or, more recently, online videos. I didn't blame them for *my* addiction, but it was a common trait in our family.

At first, my parents had a rule there would be no screens during family meals. But as we grew older and they became busier, that changed, because we all ate at different times, separately. Mom worked the night shift at the ER, Dad was out performing surgeries all day, and my sister was away at medical school. Hence, often I ate alone with my phone for company. Even when we ate together at the family dining table, we had our devices on most of the time because we were used to it.

However, my parents pursued other hobbies that took them away from their phones. My mother swam whenever she was free, and my father ran marathons. My sister and I swam, too, but I'd quit the sport recently.

We also went on a few camping trips every year together as a family, leaving all devices at home. We let the beauty of nature entertain us. I used to love these trips, particularly hiking on long trails with my camera, but on the most recent one, I sneaked my phone and watched videos I had downloaded, the whole time refusing to do anything else. That's when I realized I was an addict. And this needed to change.

I tried to stop listening to the women talk about online videos and concentrate on the book I was reading. But it took every ounce of my willpower not to get up and join them.

I sighed and shook my head. This was going to be a long and arduous journey.

***

I swore under my breath for the umpteenth time since I boarded the aircraft. What was I thinking, requesting a window seat when I knew my six foot four frame wouldn't fit? I thought I could pass the time watching the clouds, but my interest lasted for less than five minutes. Just like my attention to the thriller novel in my hand. I envied the passengers next to me, who were engrossed in the movie playing on the inflight entertainment system. Not wanting to break my resolve, I had refused the earphones the flight attendant had provided everyone.

Technically, Mr. and Mrs. Hong had not banned inflight entertainment, and I could still use it. But wouldn't that mean I'd failed to stay away from screens even for one day? And how would I survive two entire weeks? However, the cell phone rehab program would have activities to keep us occupied, right? Their ad showed people having fun playing board games, participating in team-building sports, and going sightseeing. That's what had attracted me to the program in the first place.

Convinced that it was alright, I requested the earphones and switched on the monitor in front of me. But the screen was frozen on a kids' show. No matter how many times I pressed on the "x" button to close it, it wouldn't budge. I attempted restarting the system, but it was stuck. For the next hour, I tried everything: tapping on the monitor, pressing on it and releasing, and changing the volume.

Nothing. Worked.

The passenger sitting next to me felt sorry for me and tried to fix it. However, he was also unsuccessful and got back to his own movie. I called the flight attendant, who apologized profusely for the inconvenience, and promised to get me some extra dessert to compensate.

I was tempted to make conversation with the kind passenger who had helped me earlier, but he didn't look my way at all. His eyes were glued to his screen. I sighed and racked my brain for ideas to kill the time. I decided to jot down some ways in the new pocket notebook I had bought for this trip.

It was an ordeal to reach my back pocket for the diary. If I got up too much, my head would hit the air conditioning vent above me, and if I didn't, my hand would get stuck. After what seemed like hours, I finally fished it out. I pulled the tiny pen from its compartment and started writing.

Ways to keep myself busy during the flight:

1. Peek at everyone's screen and see if I can identify what they're watching.

2. Eat really slowly. Savor every bite.

3. Read the free travel magazine in my seat pocket.

4. ~~Read the novel.~~ No, save it for later. I need to kill two weeks.

5. ~~Drink wine and fall asleep.~~ No, I don't drink.

6. Self-reflect.

7. Sleep.

I played with my retractable pen, enjoying its clicky sound, until I felt the passenger next to me tap on my shoulder. I stopped immediately and mumbled an apology.

"Do you want to switch seats for a while?" he asked. "You can use my earphones and inflight entertainment system."

I was touched by this thoughtful stranger's words, but I declined politely. "No, thank you. I'm good."

"I noticed you don't have a cell phone," he pointed out, removing his spectacles and cleaning them with a soft lens cloth. "Did you lose it?"

I shook my head. "Actually, I'm traveling without it. By choice."

"Oh, wow. Are you serious? In this day and age?"

I nodded. "I've signed up for Mobile Rehab. Are you interested in watching their viral ad?"

Immediately, he connected his phone to the flight Wi-Fi and loaded the advertisement. He let out a low whistle when it finished playing. "I should enroll our entire family in this program. I paid through the nose for the aircraft internet service for the four of us: my wife and my kids. We can't stay unplugged for a few hours, and you're doing it for two weeks?"

I smiled sheepishly, not mentioning that only teens aged sixteen to nineteen qualified for the program. "I hope I succeed."

"I'm sure you will. The Hong couple seem nice, and the venue looks like a luxurious resort with all kinds of fun activities. That should make it easier to pass the time without any screens. Good luck. I'm David, by the way. It's nice to meet you."

I shook his hand and chatted for a few minutes before he went back to his movie. Now that my neighbor knew I was off mobile devices, it felt awkward to peek into everyone's screens to guess what they were watching. Food wasn't here yet either, so I browsed the travel magazine in the seat pocket.

I got bored within a few minutes, because there were only ads in the magazine. I sighed and closed my eyes to reflect on why nothing other than my phone interested me anymore. But my mind was blank. There was nothing in there. I begged my brain to give me thoughts and memories to reflect on, but it was completely empty.

Within fifteen minutes, I had run out of things to do. Now, I had no choice but to sleep. I closed my eyes, not sleepy at all. How did people do this in the olden days? How did they manage without cell phones and social media? How were they entertained? I was going crazy.

I opened my pocket notebook again and started drawing. I sketched a dinosaur like I used to when I was a child. I drew my favorite Tyrannosaurus rex, with its short arms, sharp teeth, and ferocious eyes. I enjoyed myself as I fine-tuned the picture to make it look real. I was proud of my work when it was complete. I was no artist, but it felt wonderful to do something I loved after such a long time.

I made a mental note to buy more notebooks later, because I knew all the pages of this one would be filled by the end of the flight.

Two weeks without my phone didn't sound like such a bad idea, after all.

CHAPTER 2

Keira

I felt my heart beating rapidly in my chest from nervousness and excitement as the flight prepared to land in the Hong Kong International Airport. For a moment, I forgot that I had left my phone at home and focused on the mesmerizing turquoise blue sea that glistened in the sunlight. As we descended, a small island appeared. I got a bird's eye view of giant skyscrapers that hid the ground beneath them. Then the passenger in the window seat leaned forward and blocked me from seeing anything further.

When we landed, the first sounds I heard were those of notification beeps on the passengers' phones. Instinctively, I reached into my pocket to get mine out, before I remembered I didn't have it. My smartphone was in my dorm room. I had taken off to the airport in a huff, too angry to think straight.

"This is all your fault, Diego Garcia," I said in a low tone with my fists clenched.

Diego and I had been seeing each other for the last three years. We were in the same class in high school and became good friends really fast. We started a band with our friends, which brought us closer together, and eventually we started dating. Since then, we'd been together as bandmates *and* boyfriend-girlfriend.

Until...

"I still can't believe that you were cheating on me, Diego," I whispered to myself. "I saw you kiss someone else with my own eyes."

Someone tapped my shoulder, bringing me back to the present with a jolt. "Excuse me, but I need to get my bag."

"Sorry," I mumbled and got up from my aisle seat, hoping I hadn't spoken too loudly.

I removed my carry-on luggage from the overhead bin and exited the aircraft. After exchanging Brazilian real for Hong Kong dollars, and retrieving my checked bag, I trudged toward the counter labeled "Octopus Card," where there was a long line. Octopus card was a pre-paid card that made traveling and shopping in Hong Kong hassle-free. While waiting, I could hardly keep my eyes open, because I hadn't slept on the flight at all.

I reached for the wet tissue they'd provided on the airline and dabbed my eyes with it.

"Next," yelled the customer service representative to gain the attention of a tall white guy who was too busy talking to a shorter Asian man.

"Sir, do you need an Octopus card or not?" the rep asked, losing her patience. "There are people waiting in line."

"Sorry, I'll get a card please," the tall guy responded.

"We'll reimburse the amount," the shorter man assured him, while they waited for the pass. "It's likely you won't need the card, because our organization will drive you around the city when needed. But if you get separated from the group, or get lost, you'll have an alternate mode of transport to reach the hotel safely. It's the best option since you won't have your phone."

I wondered why someone purposely wouldn't bring their phone to a busy city like Hong Kong. Maybe they had their reasons, like me. It would be hard to survive, particularly if they didn't know the languages. I observed how most of the local people used their devices to make payments and gain access to metro entrances. How was I going to get by without mine?

"How many cards do you need?" the customer service representative asked when it was finally my turn.

"I already bought a card online," I answered. "Can you please check?"

"I need the receipt."

"Sorry, I left my phone at home. My receipt was in that."

She shook her head. "No receipt, no card. You have to buy another one."

"Can't you search for my name or email address? Please?"

"No, sorry. I don't have the facility to do that. You can buy a new one now and request a refund for the old one when you get back home. Do you want to do that?"

I sighed reluctantly. "Alright, I'll get a new one." I handed her a wad of cash I'd drawn earlier. "Please load it up as well."

"Let me pay for her new card." The Asian man from earlier, who had stepped aside when it was my turn, handed the cash to the representative before I could protest. "It's not correct to charge the young lady again. What will she think of our country?"

"No, I can't let you do that," I said, trying to pay him back.

"It's fine, ma'am," he replied, refusing the money. "Welcome to Hong Kong."

"It's not alright," I insisted. "You don't need to pay for me. I don't even know you."

"Ma'am, you're holding up the line. Please take your card and leave." That was the customer sales representative.

I followed the Asian man, who walked with the tall guy toward the airport exit. "Sir, what you did was not right. Please let me pay you back."

"Why don't you buy me a cup of coffee instead?" he asked.

I didn't like this at all. I had no idea who this man was or why he paid for my Octopus card. And I didn't want to buy him a cup of coffee or make conversation. But he had a persuasive approach that was almost impossible to refuse.

"So, you don't have your phone?" he asked.

I shook my head but didn't say anything.

"Do you have a hotel booking? Where are you staying?"

I had had it with this strange man and his inquisitive questions.

I took a deep breath. "Look, I really don't want to talk to you. And I didn't like it that you paid for my card. So, I'll buy you your coffee, and let's go our respective ways."

"Sorry, it's just that I couldn't help but overhear that you don't have a mobile device. It's difficult to survive without one in a busy country like this." He paused for effect. "If you don't have accommodation. I can help you." He placed his hand on the shoulder of the tall guy, who had his headphones on. "Mr. Matthews is staying at our hotel. You can ask him."

Mr. Matthews nodded. "Yes. He's a part of the Mobile Rehab. It's an organization that helps people who can't be without their mobile devices." He turned to the shorter man. "Show her the brochure."

I went through the brochure, which had photos of a lavish hotel room with two queen-sized beds and a swanky leather couch. The attached bathroom was furnished with a luxurious Jacuzzi tub with an overhead and handheld shower. There was an on-site recreation room with modern gym equipment, an indoor swimming pool, and even table tennis.

My favorite photograph was that of a large bookshelf stacked with all kinds of books and board games. The cozy reading corner had bean bags, stools, and other comfortable chairs and tables for people to read and play. I could easily spend hours in there.

I exclaimed when I saw the price. I thought I wouldn't be able to afford it, but it was less than the hotel room I'd booked for the week.

"The only rule for using these facilities is that you can't have any mobile devices on you," the Asian man said. "And you have to arrange your own meals. But that's not a problem, because there are many options that are a short walk away from the hotel. Are you interested?"

I shook my head. "I already have a hotel reservation, thanks."

"No problem."

"Do you have a printout of your booking confirmation?" the tall guy, Mr. Matthews, asked me. "Or is that on your phone too?"

"I haven't paid yet," I said. I looked down, feeling stupid. "And no, I don't have a paper receipt."

"What if they refuse to give you your room key?" he asked.

"And is there a room cancelation fee?" the Mobile Rehab employee added.

"No. They don't have a no-show charge either," I replied.

"Then you should join us," the tall guy said, smiling. "I'm Rory Matthews, and this is Mr. Hong, cofounder of the Mobile Rehab. There will be more people with us for the program. It'll be a good opportunity to connect with people our age from across the world. The rehab is particularly for kids between sixteen and nineteen years old."

Rory's smile reached his warm brown eyes and lit up his entire face. He seemed like a pleasant guy, about the same age as me. Despite the tiring journey, he was well-groomed with a neat day-old stubble. Not a single strand of his wavy dark brown hair was out of place. He towered over almost everyone in the airport with his six foot plus, lean and muscular frame. He was most probably either a model or an athlete.

"Are you going to pay now?" Mr. Hong asked. "We accept only cash."

"How is it possible that your hotel rooms are so big?" I asked back. "Space is scarce in Hong Kong."

Mr. Hong nodded. "You are correct. However, this is a newer area in the city. It's not fully commercialized yet."

"Let's sit down somewhere and talk," I said. "I have more questions."

"We need to make it quick, though," Mr. Hong replied. "Two people are already waiting in my shuttle."

"It won't take long. Why don't you get a table? I'll get your coffee in the meantime."

I paid for Mr. Hong's beverage and thought about his offer while I waited. I read the terms and conditions in fine print to ensure this wasn't a scam. I carried the hot cup of coffee back to the table where Rory and Mr. Hong were waiting for me.

Mr. Hong sipped his coffee. "So, you had some questions for me?"

"Yes. What if there's an emergency? How will we contact anyone without our phones?"

"There is a landline in your room. You can make calls from there, provided you pay for them."

"Is there a way to contact you?"

Mr. Hong handed me his business card. "My wife and I are available twenty-four hours a day. Call us if you need anything at all. But remember, this is a landline too. We both have a strict no smartphone policy. You can leave us a voicemail if we are not around, and we will return your call as soon as we can."

"Alright, I'm in," I said, taking the cash out of my wallet. "I need a receipt though."

Mr. Hong printed the amount on a piece of paper, signed it, and gave it to me. "Here you go."

We exited the airport, dragging our suitcases behind us. After walking for fifteen minutes, we reached the parking lot where a green shuttle waited for us. A lady, who I recognized as Mrs. Hong from the brochure, helped us place our luggage on the rack. Two people, a boy and a girl, about my age, were already in the vehicle. They were fast asleep, probably exhausted from their journeys. Both were snoring softly.

I felt my own eyelids close but forced them wide open. What if Mr. and Mrs. Hong were abducting us? In the latest episode of my favorite crime series, *Forensix*, a serial killer held an entire family hostage in a van like this. Was I in a similar situation? I still didn't trust these strangers. Did Rory feel the same way?

I turned around to see Rory stretched out in the backseat. Poor guy. How uncomfortable must he have felt flying economy class—I knew because I'd seen his luggage tag—on a long international flight? At just five foot six, I found it difficult. These were the times I wished I was shorter.

He smiled and waved. I grinned back, relieved that he didn't look tense. Just then, I realized I hadn't introduced myself. When I was about to get up to do so, Mrs. Hong hurried to Rory's seat.

"This is the reimbursement for your Octopus card," Mrs. Hong said, giving Rory a few crisp notes of Hong Kong dollars. "As mentioned in our brochure, the card price is on us, but you need to load it with the amount you need."

Seeing this, I relaxed a little. Mr. and Mrs. Hong were nice people. They weren't criminals. I was safe in this shuttle.

I slid toward the window near my seat and opened it. The gentle breeze blowing on my face and the vehicle's motion made me fall into a blissful sleep.

CHAPTER 3

Rory

I was the only one awake on the shuttle. Though I hadn't slept at all on the plane, I felt energetic. I was also excited about spending time with the other three. My stomach growled with hunger, and I realized I hadn't eaten much. I had eaten all my meals on the flight, but that was ages ago. I opened my bag and munched on a protein bar.

The shuttle came to a stop in front of a tall building. It was a skyscraper in the true sense of the word, because the top of the building was covered by clouds. The weather in this city changed within minutes. It was bright and sunny when we landed, but now it looked like it was about to rain.

"We've arrived at our destination," Mrs. Hong announced. "Please wait inside the hotel lobby. Mr. Hong and I will bring your luggage. Mr. Tan has the key to your suite."

"That's me." The other guy in our group raised his hand. "I'm Desmond Tan."

Desmond looked like a movie star with a flawlessly symmetrical face and short black hair. He offered his hand for me to shake, and I noticed it was soft, warm, and perfectly manicured. I made a mental note to ask him which brand of hand lotion he used.

"And I'm Champa Naidu. Nice to meet you."

That was the other girl in our group, the one I hadn't met yet. She had tied her long, silky, straight black hair up in a loose ponytail with several strands falling freely on her pretty face.

"And my name is Keira Delgado," said the girl with nape-length curly brown hair and gorgeous brown eyes. "I just realized I haven't introduced myself yet, though we met earlier at the airport, Rory."

I laughed. "That's fine. It's nice to meet all of you."

We got down from the bus and walked toward the hotel. Within two minutes, we reached the lobby, which was crowded. There was no place to sit or stand. Feeling suffocated, the four of us decided to wait outside on the sidewalk. But there were too many people there as well.

Even after waiting for over a half an hour, there was no sign of the Hongs. So we decided to look for the couple. Keira went back to the place where the shuttle had pulled over, and I searched the entire street. Desmond headed to the lobby, and Champa stayed put in case Mr. Hong arrived.

I returned to our waiting area first, followed shortly by Keira. Neither of us had seen the Hongs or their shuttle. Desmond came back after twenty minutes, and we looked at him hopefully. He didn't say anything, but simply gestured for us to follow him, and we did so, unable to bear the suspense any longer.

After what seemed like an eternity, we reached a quieter area on the lobby floor, and Desmond finally spoke. "I have good news and bad news. Which one do you want to hear first?"

"Please. Just tell us everything, Des," Champa retorted. "We are getting anxious now."

Desmond cleared his throat. "So, the good news is, I found our luggage. It was left at the entrance. And the bad news is that we have been duped."

"What do you mean by duped?" I asked.

"We should have guessed something was wrong when we entered the building earlier," Desmond said, not answering my question.

Keira frowned. "What do you mean?"

"What was the name of the hotel in the Mobile Rehab advertisements?"

"Hotel Grand Luxury," we answered in unison.

Desmond nodded. "Yes. Did you see that name anywhere outside this building? It was in prominent gold letters in the ad."

We shook our heads mutely.

He continued. "This building is a hotel and a residential complex. A few floors are rented out to hotel guests and on the others, there are apartments."

"So, that means our suite could be in this hotel, correct?" Keira asked.

Desmond shook his head. "No. We have a key, one that fits a lock. All the other hotel guests are carrying key cards."

"So, where will we stay tonight?" I asked, knowing it was a rhetorical question.

Desmond dangled the key Mrs. Hong had given him in front of us. "This is not a key to the hotel suite we were promised. We need to find out what it's for, *if* it's real."

"Is there a number on the key?" Keira asked. She seemed calm, considering the situation.

"Yes, but no one knows where that is in this twenty-five-floor building," Desmond replied.

Champa examined the keys closely. "The number is 2601."

"But there are only twenty-five floors," I stated.

Desmond nodded. "Exactly."

"How about we go up to the topmost floor?" Champa suggested. "Maybe there are stairs for the twenty-sixth floor."

Though the idea seemed promising, it was an ordeal to get on the elevator. There were too many people waiting, and the capacity was limited. And climbing twenty-six flights of stairs seemed like a nightmare, especially since all four of us were ravenous.

As if she read my mind, Champa reached into her backpack, brought out four big chocolate bars and gave one to each to us.

"You're a lifesaver, Champs." Desmond spoke with his mouth full. "Bless you for feeding hungry people."

Champa laughed. "Remind me to refill our emergency stash."

"I have protein bars," I said.

Keira unzipped her backpack. "I have potato chips."

"And I'll pay for dinner tonight," Desmond offered.

We finished all the snacks within minutes, feeling temporarily satiated.

"Who's up for a trek up twenty-six flights of stairs?" I asked.

The other three groaned in unison. "Are you serious?"

"Well, we do need a place to sleep tonight."

Just as we were about to enter the stairway, the elevator doors opened, and we bolted toward it at lightning speed. There wasn't even space to breathe, but at least we would reach the upper floor faster. Or so we thought. It stopped on every floor, and we had to press the "close" button each time. To make things worse, the automatic door system was broken, and it would close and reopen at least five times before proceeding to the next floor.

After what seemed like an eternity, we finally reached the twenty-fifth floor. We ran up the stairs to the topmost floor, hoping for the best.

"We're doomed," Desmond cried. "There's no apartment or room here. There's just one door that probably leads to the rooftop area, and it's locked."

Champa squeezed his hand reassuringly. "We can't give up hope. There must be some way."

"Maybe we can try the second floor," I suggested. "2601 starts with two."

Keira shrugged. "There's no harm in trying."

"But what if it doesn't work?" Desmond asked. "Shouldn't we have a contingency plan?"

"Well, I don't have enough cash on me to pay for a hotel for another two weeks," I replied. "Rescheduling an airline ticket will also cost a lot. So I can't go back home."

Keira nodded. "Same here. I spent most of my money on the so-called rehab."

"We don't have our phones either," Champa reminded us. "That limits our search options. It's already eight in the evening."

"Let's do one thing at a time," Desmond said. "Otherwise, we'll all just panic, which won't help our situation."

We decided to go down to the second floor to try our luck one last time. No one spoke on our way downstairs. Everyone was probably praying for a miracle. When we reached our destination, we went in different directions as planned.

All the apartment numbers started with "26," which was promising. But 2601 was nowhere to be found. We checked many times together and separately, but there was no 2601.

"Who starts counting from 2602?" I wailed.

Desmond shook his head. "I know, right? How lame is that?"

"Guys, I think we found it," Champa shouted from one of the corners.

"I'm sure I see the numbers written with a piece of chalk on this door," Keira said. "Desmond, can you bring the key?"

Desmond and I ran as fast as we could toward the girls. We also saw the numbers two, six, zero, and one written on the door with a piece of chalk along with a sign board that read, "Domestic Help."

I could feel the tension building up as Desmond inserted the key into the padlock attached to an old-fashioned latch. When we heard the sound of the latch opening, followed by a creaking noise, all four of us collapsed on the floor in relief.

Forget luxury and comfort. We were just extremely thankful we didn't have to sleep on the streets tonight.

***

We were pleasantly surprised to see that the tiny apartment was squeaky clean, without even a speck of dirt in sight. There were hardly a few inches of space left, though, when all four of us stood with our bags in the living room. And the kitchenette could fit only two people at a time.

"Guys, look. There's another room here," Keira called out to us.

Champa went inside, but Desmond and I had to stay in the living room, because it couldn't fit more than two of us.

Suddenly, Desmond burst into laughter. He held his stomach and shook uncontrollably. Champa followed suit. Soon, Keira and I were in splits too. Though I had no idea why. Their laughter was too infectious.

Once we all calmed down, Desmond finally spoke. "How did we believe that this busy city, where space is precious, had an affordable hotel suite with two queen beds *and* a couch?"

Champa did a facepalm gesture, lightly slapping her forehead. "How dumb of us."

I sighed. "I got carried away by their ad. I didn't want to see the reality."

Keira chuckled. "And I thought I was smart for reading the terms and conditions. I even asked so many questions."

We shook our heads and laughed again. Even though we felt stupid for getting conned, at least we saw the lighter side of the situation.

For the next few minutes, we explored the little space we would call home during our stay here. It was better than I imagined. There were four futons, two in the bedroom and two in the living room. We decided the boys would take the bedroom and the girls would sleep in the living room.

The kitchen cabinets were stocked with instant noodles, bread, eggs, condiments like ketchup and mustard, and basic spices, such as salt and pepper. There were two pans and just enough plates, bowls, and cutlery for the four of us. The small kitchen even had a refrigerator, microwave oven, electric kettle, toaster, and a stove.

The bathroom was tiny with hardly any space to shower. The toilet and sink were also smaller than usual. However, there was a small cupboard under the sink with cleaning supplies.

"This place isn't bad at all," said Keira. "It's almost as if the Hong couple felt guilty for lying to us."

"Wow, there's even a landline," Champa exclaimed.

Desmond laughed. "I bet it doesn't work. Try Mr. Hong's number."

Keira dialed the number listed on his business card. "This phone is out of order."

"Can we at least call the emergency helpline, if needed?" I asked.

"Hopefully," Keira answered. "I don't want to try now and get fined, though. We've lost enough money already."

Desmond's stomach growled loudly, and I was reminded of my own hunger. "Goodness, it's getting late for dinner. If we don't hurry, we won't eat tonight."

"I need proper food," said Desmond, locking the door from outside. "A measly snack isn't going to cut it this time. No offense to the three of you who were kind enough to feed me earlier."

We laughed and hurried down the stairs. As expected, the restaurant on-site was too crowded. We decided to explore a less busy diner in the area. But they all had wait times of over an hour. Most were closing soon.

Most of the eateries had their menus outside for their customers' benefit. While most of them had the full menu, some only had a QR code. We had to rule the latter out for obvious reasons.

"Um, I'm vegetarian," said Keira softly. "None of these places seem to have anything without meat. It's alright. I'll eat the instant noodles when we get back."

"No, there are only two small packets of meatless instant noodles," I replied. "That won't be enough for you."

Champa placed a hand lightly on Keira's shoulder. "I eat chicken and fish, but only occasionally. I'm perfectly fine eating vegetarian or vegan meals. So, you'll always have company."

"I'll eat anything right now," Desmond declared. "I just want food."

My stomach growled. "We need to hurry. The only less-crowded place on this street is closing in twenty minutes."

"Let's try our luck in four different restaurants on this street," Keira suggested. "We will meet back here in about five minutes."

"None of you are wearing a watch," I pointed out. "How will you tell the time?"

Keira laughed. "You're right. I hadn't thought about that."

"There's a large wall clock outside the building adjacent to ours," Champa said. "We can use that."

We agreed and went our own ways. Boldly, I entered the tiny diner that was about to close soon. This had one vegetarian option on their menu. The aroma of hot meals that wafted through the air made my mouth water. I was tempted to barge into the kitchen and gobble up all the leftovers.

I rang the bell on the cashier counter, and an elderly woman wearing an apron came outside.

"Sorry, we are about to close."

I bowed slightly, not letting her curt tone bother me. "I understand, ma'am. But my friends and I were hoping you could at least pack us some leftover vegetarian fried rice. Two of my friends don't eat meat, and there are no other diners close by with meatless options. Besides, your restaurant seems like the best one."

"Are you new to the city?" she asked, relaxing a little. "We close early in this area."

I nodded. "We just arrived a few hours ago."

Her expression softened further, so I continued. "None of us have our cell phones. So, we can't even order food or travel outside the area without getting lost."

She shook her head and sighed. "Oh, you're staying in the Hongs' house."

For a moment, she seemed lost in her thoughts, so I waited patiently for her to speak again.

"Bring your friends. I'll cook you all a hot meal," she said.

Delighted, I squealed like a child. "Thank you so much. I can't express how grateful we are."

"But I can only make one dish. Okay?"

I nodded vigorously. "No problem."

She laughed, amused at my excitement. "How many of you?"

"Four," I answered. "But, please, prepare food enough for at least six people. We are all starving."

She smiled, amused. "Sure. But please change the sign on the door to 'closed' when you bring your friends inside."

I agreed, thanked her profusely again, and ran to meet the others.

We would have a hot meal on our table and a shelter above our heads tonight.

After everything we had gone through today, this felt like a lottery prize!

Chapter 4

Keira

Champa, Desmond, and I threw ourselves on Rory and hugged him tightly—with his consent, of course—when he announced he had managed to convince the diner owner to prepare a hot meal for us. All three of us had been turned down. Dejected, we had purchased snacks in the 24/7 convenience store across the street.

Desmond raised the snack bag and showed it to Rory. "These chips and cookies would've been our dinner if not for you. You saved our lives. Tell me what you want in return. Should I ask my father to add your name in his will? I can do that."

The rest of us laughed.

"I'm serious, guys," Desmond replied.

Champa nudged Rory. "His father is rich. Don't miss this chance."

Rory chuckled. "The hot meal is reward enough for now. I don't need anything else."

"Then, I will grant you a wish," Desmond declared dramatically. "Name anything you want. This offer is open for the rest of our time here."

We would have teased Desmond more, but the aroma of the piping hot meal as we entered the small diner mesmerized us. The eatery had six small tables, surrounded by four chairs each. If all twenty-four seats were filled, the place would be packed, leaving no space for anyone to breathe. The paint on the walls had worn out, and the floor looked really old. Near the entrance, there were party streamers with a board that read "Celebrating Lau's Cosy Haven's 37th Birthday" with last month's date.

"The food must be really good here," I murmured to myself. "Otherwise, there's no way this old place would have survived for almost four decades."

Rory, Desmond, and Champa were staring at the kitchen entrance in silence, waiting for our food. Soon, the owner brought a huge wok filled with delicious fried rice in one hand and four plates in the other.

She set the wok on the table next to us and placed the plates in front of us. "Do you want me to serve you?"

We all nodded eagerly.

Once our plates were each filled with a heap of the fried rice, I dug in right away, not caring that it burned my mouth. I cried out in pleasure at the savory umami flavors that burst into my mouth. I was moved by the amount of thought the chef had put into making this. There were umpteen veggies and other lip-smacking ingredients, and it didn't feel like a leftover dish at all.

Everyone ate in silence, and within minutes, we had polished off our plates and the entire wok was clean. I blinked back the tears in my eyes, grateful for the wonderful meal. I would never, ever forget this restaurant or the kind lady who went out of her way to feed us. If not for her, I would have had to go to bed on an almost empty stomach.

"I've never enjoyed a meal as much as I did today." Desmond voiced everyone's feelings. He added after a pause, "I'm a picky eater. I don't eat broccoli, bok choy, yu choy, and mushrooms. And I'm not a fan of tofu. But today, I was not only grateful to have food on my plate, but I thoroughly enjoyed every bite."

"Are you open to trying newer dishes now?" Champa teased.

Desmond nodded vehemently in agreement.

"Do you know each other?" I asked.

Champa nodded. "Yes. We go to the same high school in Canada. Des is my best friend."

"Hey, I live in Canada, too," Rory replied. "I'm a university student."

"Same here," I said. "I go to college too. In Brazil."

The four of us sat in awkward silence. I wanted to ask the others more questions about themselves, but they didn't seem to be in a chatty mood.

"We need to pay and leave," Rory said, glancing at his watch. "It's way past closing time for this restaurant."

When we were about to get up, the owner stopped us. "Have some dessert before you go. This is on the house."

She placed four bowls of silken tofu pudding in front of us. We savored the decadent dessert that melted in our mouths, not worrying how odd our moans of pleasure sounded. The sweet treat was like a warm, comforting hug for everything we went through today.

We thanked Mrs. Lau, the owner, profusely for the scrumptious meal. As promised, Desmond paid the bill, along with a generous tip. Mrs. Lau refused to take the extra cash, no matter how many times he offered. She just wanted us to come back during our stay here.

We walked back to our apartment in silence. Everyone had a satisfied smile on their face. Suddenly, I felt a terrible pain in my ear. Air travel made my ears hurt, and I needed my ear drops badly. Wait, had I packed them?

"Are you alright?" Champa asked.

"I think I forgot to bring my ear drops," I replied softly. "I didn't realize it until now."

She gave me an empathetic look. "Are your ears hurting because of the flight?"

I nodded.

"Let's see if we can find one at the convenience store that's open all night. I'll go with you."

I smiled gratefully. "Thanks." I turned to the guys. "We're going to the store. Do you want to come?"

"Yes, I'm headed there," Rory answered.

"I need to use the restroom urgently," Desmond said. "I'll head back to the apartment."

"It's best we don't go alone anywhere," I said. "We don't have any way to communicate with each other."

"Keira, let's go to the store together," Rory suggested. "Champa, why don't you accompany Desmond?"

"Are you sure you'll be okay?" Champa whispered.

I nodded. "Yes, thanks."

She patted my hand lightly. "Let me know if I can help in any way. My sister has sensitive ears too."

I was grateful that she cared, even though we had met only a few hours ago. "I will, thanks."

***

After Champa and Desmond left, Rory and I walked to the convenience store. The night breeze was slightly chilly, and I wore my hood. I placed my hands inside my pockets, surprised to see Rory removing his jacket and tying it around his waist. It was windy, and it looked like it was about to rain.

"Aren't you cold?" I asked, knowing it was a stupid question.

Rory laughed and shook his head. "I'm from Canada." He untied his jacket from his waist and extended it to me. "You can wear this if you want."

I smiled. "I'm good, thanks. I have another jacket in my backpack. It gets cold in Brazil too. But I can't handle it very well. So, I'm always equipped."

"Cool. We're almost there anyway."

When we were about to enter the shop, a woman ran out, as if she had seen a ghost. She was in such a hurry, she nearly knocked over the bright green sign outside the door.

"Go somewhere else," she warned. "That old man is crazy."

Rory and I looked at each other, puzzled as we went inside.

"Hello, sir, madam. How can I help you?" the cashier, an elderly man in his seventies or eighties asked, getting up from his seat.

We were surprised. It was uncommon for a cashier of a convenience store to greet customers, particularly when it was so busy. At least ten people were waiting in the checkout line.

"We're just looking around," Rory answered.

"Are you new around here?" the cashier asked. "I've never seen you before."

"We just arrived today," I replied.

"Where are you from? How did you arrive? Which airline? Business or economy class? Which hotel are you staying?"

"Can you please let us pass, sir?" Rory requested politely, seemingly unaffected by the old man's interrogation.

He shook his head. "I read that it's important to know your customer. That's what I'm doing."

I was amused by this man, who took "know your customer" literally, but I didn't want to answer any of his questions.

"Excuse me, Grandpa, can you please help us here? It's getting late," one of the customers called to him, and he reluctantly went back to work.

Now I knew why the lady had warned us against entering this place. The inquisitive cashier lacked the concept of personal space. Though he was out of our sight, we could hear him trouble other customers.

"Why have you bought gluten-free bread? Are you allergic? Or is someone else in your family? Is it celiac or something else? How bad is it?"

"Why do you want to know? Are you going to write my autobiography?" one of the customers, also an elderly person, retorted angrily.

Rory snorted, failing to hold back his laughter as he continued shopping.

"It's important for us to know our customers, ma'am," the cashier replied, sounding unfazed. "The customer is the king."

I went into an uncontrollable fit of silent giggles, tears streaming from my eyes. Rory's snorts grew louder, which he unsuccessfully tried to hide by coughing. We were laughing at another customer's expense, knowing that it would be our turn to face the cashier's inquisitive questions in a few minutes.

As I searched for the ear drops, I continued listening to the entertaining conversations between the cashier and other customers. Most of them gave one-word answers or just said "no English" and "no Chinese." But the funniest was the one who answered "huh?" to everything the cashier asked.

"But, ma'am, you were able to hear yesterday. How did you lose your ability today?"

"She got hit by a hippopotamus," someone else answered, their voice dripping in sarcasm.

I bit my tongue hard, not wanting to be rude and erupt into laughter again.

"Oh no. Did you go to the hospital? Which one did you go to? How much was the bill? Do you have insurance? Which one? Are you wearing hearing aids?"

"I'm back from my break," a male voice interrupted him. "Grandpa, Dad wants you back home immediately. He asked me to inform you."

"Yuan, thank goodness you're back," the customer exclaimed. "I don't have to pretend to be deaf anymore."

Yuan seemed to be the same age as us, maybe a year or two younger.

"Sorry, I came back as quickly as I could," Yuan said.

"It's okay, son. We know how hard you work. At least you deserve to eat in peace."

They continued chatting in Chinese for a while. I wondered why the elderly man spoke in English with the local customers. I had read that many people in Hong Kong could converse in English but preferred their native languages.

"I hope your grandfather goes back to London to your aunt's place. He talks too much."

Yuan pretended not to hear the rude comment. "Come on, let me help you, so you can enjoy the rest of your evening."

He was very fast and efficient, and before we knew it, it was our turn.

"Did you find everything you needed today?" he asked as he scanned Rory's colored pencils and sketchbook.

"Do you have ear drops?" I asked as Rory paid for his items.

Yuan shook his head. "No, sorry. We don't have it here. You can try this store though." He handed us a piece of paper with the address and the bus number. "It's the first stop after this, if you take the bus."

"Thanks."

Yuan smiled. "I hope you have a pleasant stay in our city."

Rory and I exited the store, and I contemplated whether it was worth the effort to go to another shop. It was almost ten, not the best time to roam outside.

"Let's go back home, Rory," I said. "I can manage without the ear drops."

"Are you sure? The bus stop is very close by."

I nodded. "It's getting late."

All of a sudden, it started pouring heavily. Both of us ran to the bus stop for shelter. Rory removed his coat from his waist and put it on, covering his head with its hood. The intensity of the rain was too much, making it impossible to see the roads or the sidewalk.

I sighed loudly. "Everything that could go wrong today, already did. What else is left?"

CHAPTER 5

Rory

I swore under my breath, now wearing my waterproof jacket, regretting my decision to set foot in this country without my cell phone. I'd been duped, even though I had read all the reviews and studied every single letter on the so-called "Mobile Rehab" website. And now, this. I had escaped from my chaotic life back home, hoping to get some peace in a foreign land. But here I was, in a bigger mess.

I took a deep breath to calm my mind. There was no point in getting worked up. I had to focus on getting back to the apartment. I looked at Keira, who seemed to be in a lot of discomfort and was rubbing her ears constantly. I felt sorry for her. Maybe the rain was a sign that she should get the ear drops.

"Let's just get on the bus and buy your stuff," I suggested to Keira.

She nodded. "We can't walk back to the hotel anyway."

The intensity of the rain increased further as we ran to the bus approaching the stop. Yuan had told us that any bus would drop us at our destination.

Soon, we reached the big supermarket, and Keira found what she needed. Here, too, there was a long line at the cashier's counter with no self-checkout options.

While standing in the line, a couple started fighting loudly in English.

"Why do you have to create a scene in public?" the husband demanded. "Can't you wait until we get back to the hotel?"

"You're the one who kept asking me what happened," the wife retorted.

"That's because you gave me the cold shoulder the whole trip. I'm sick of walking on eggshells around you. This is supposed to be our holiday, and you're ruining it."

"No. You're the one destroying my life. I told you I was fine, you nag."

"Oh yeah? You barely spoke two words to me the last two days. It's as if I don't exist."

You're overreacting as usual, Rory.

"Rory? Earth to Rory," I heard a faint voice say. "Hey, Rory, are you okay?"

I jerked out of my reverie and realized I'd gone down memory lane watching the couple argue. I felt my chest constricting and my heart palpitating. I hoped my distress wasn't visible on my face and pretended to yawn.

"I'm fine, Keira. Just tired and sleepy. Did you get your ear drops?"

Keira raised the shopping bag in her hand with a bright smile on her face. "Yes. I finally got them. And I also bought some other stuff."

"Awesome. Now, let's get back home."

We exited the store and ran to the bus stop as it was still raining heavily. Luckily for us, a bus approached immediately, and we got in. Within a few minutes, we got to our stop and exited the bus.

"Was there a hotel with lion statues at the entrance near Yuan's store?" Keira asked.

I was confused. "Maybe there was one on the opposite side of the road. I didn't really pay attention."

Keira pointed to a brightly lit neon sign in the shape of a large coffee cup. "Was there a twenty-four-hour café? I don't think we would have missed that."

I was a little annoyed at Keira's questions. "What's your point?"

"We got down at the wrong stop."

I looked around, desperately hoping Keira was wrong. But I didn't recognize a single shop. Nor could I find Yuan's convenience store, which would have been hard to miss with its bright green board.

I sighed loudly. "You're right. We're lost."

"Now, what do we do? Wait for the next bus?"

I took a flashlight from my backpack and read the bus numbers. "Ours doesn't come here."

"Great," Keira muttered under her breath. "Why am I not surprised?"

I shook my head mirroring her distress. "We have the worst luck."

As if in agreement with my statement, a bolt of lightning flashed, followed by the booming sound of thunder. We hurried into the twenty-four-hour café for shelter. No one else seemed to be inside, not even the owner or any servers. They were probably inside the kitchen, not expecting customers during the storm.

Keira rushed to the washroom, while I rang the bell at the cashier counter, hoping someone would come outside. When there was no response, I took a seat at one of the booths near the window. I drummed my fingers on the table to distract myself from my wet pants and looked around at the orange-themed interior.

The café was small with only six tables—three booths and three tables with cane chairs. It was well-lit, with numerous focus lights on the ceiling. Matching orange paper lanterns hung from the ceiling, giving the place an ethnic feel. I got up from my seat to admire the framed paintings on the walls, depicting dragons and other enchanting creatures from Chinese folktales.

A roaring sound of thunder brought me back to reality. I wasn't here to enjoy the art, no matter how beautiful it was. I was here with a near stranger to shelter ourselves from the storm. We were lost and had to try to find a way to get back home.

I opened my backpack and removed the Hong Kong map I had brought from home. I unfolded it on the table and tried to figure out where we were.

"Hey, Rory, why don't you dry your clothes under the hand drier in the bathroom?" Keira's voice made me jump. "Sorry, I didn't mean to startle you."

"It's alright. I'm just trying to find our way back home."

"Any luck?" she asked, taking a seat opposite to mine.

I shook my head. "None, whatsoever. I think I forgot how to read a map."

Keira laughed. "We're too pampered by map apps on our phones with features like GPS and 'send my current location.'"

I nodded. "Tell me about it. Except for the airport, I can't find anything else on here."

"It's alright. I'm sure if both of us rack our brains together, we will find a way home," Keira assured. "Why don't you go and freshen up and let me take a dig at this until you're back?"

I went to the men's room, removed my wet socks, and dried myself under the hand drier. The warmth felt good on my cold feet though it was uncomfortable standing on one foot and raising the other to access the blower. Just as I was about to shift my balance on the other side, the lights went out and the sound of the dryer stopped.

There was a power cut. It was pitch dark, and I couldn't see a thing. I tried to get to the bathroom door but hit myself hard on the corner of the sink counter. I winced in pain and let out a string of profanities, loudly, not caring who could hear me.

"Are you okay?" Keira asked, knocking lightly. "I got you your flashlight."

I opened the door. "Thanks. Can you get my bag, too, please? I forgot to bring it with me."

"Here you go. I brought that too."

I grinned widely despite the situation. "That's thoughtful of you, thank you." I pointed to her backpack. "Why are you carrying that? You could have left it at the table."

Keira walked away without answering my question.

I changed into dry pants, proud of my habit of packing an extra set of clothes in my carry-on luggage, in case the airline lost my checked bag.

Feeling better, I went back to the booth, where Keira was studying the map intently under a flashlight, sipping on a steaming cup of coffee. She pinched the paper and extended her forefinger and thumb.

"That's not an app," I said, amused at her antics. "Pinch zoom isn't going to work on it."

She giggled. "I forgot about that. It's become a habit." She slid a mug of hot coffee toward me. "Here, this is yours."

I gave her a questioning look. "How did we get this?"

"Your, um, monologue earlier made the server finally realize someone was here."

I chuckled. "I'm glad my loud and inappropriate soliloquy did *some* good."

A short, middle-aged lady wearing an apron arrived at our table with two plates of egg tarts and a tea candle.

"Did you order these?" I asked Keira, pointing at the dessert.

She shook her head. "No, I didn't." She turned to our server. "Excuse me, ma'am, we didn't order these. But thank you for the candle."

The lady smiled at us and spoke in a local language, probably Cantonese. The only words I understood were "sorry" and "free," which she repeated many times while bowing.

"I think she's feeling guilty for not attending to us earlier," I whispered to Keira.

The lady pushed the plates toward us further, bowed, and left.

The freshly baked tarts looked tempting with their crispy outer shell and the soft golden yellow filling. Egg tarts were famous across Hong Kong, and people waited for hours in long lines for these treats.

"Are you going to eat that?" Keira asked.

"Sure, why not?"

She leaned forward and looked me in the eye. "What if they are drugged?"

I almost spat out my coffee. "What?"

She shrugged. "It's possible. Haven't you watched crime shows? Killers love storms."

I laughed. "Come on, they wouldn't do that in a café!"

"We're all alone here, so no witnesses. There's no power, so there wouldn't be a CCTV anywhere. And the terrible weather makes it easy for criminals to do the deed and cover it up easily," she reasoned.

"Can we please change the topic?" I asked, setting my plate aside. "You're scaring the heck out of me!"

Keira laughed. "Sure. So are we giving up on the map?" Before I could respond, she spoke again and pointed on the paper. "I found our current location. Let's mark it."

I placed a button where she was pointing. "You're right. This café is opposite Hotel Grand Shi. That's the hotel with the two big lion statues we saw earlier." I gave her another button. "Now, let's find 'home.'"

"Do you always carry extra buttons with you?" Keira asked, pointing to the tiny box in my hand.

I nodded. "I don't like my shirts missing any. So I carry the spare ones with me all the time."

"I'm impressed." She turned back to the map. "But do you remember the name of the hotel in our building or Yuan's convenience store?"

I was stumped by Keira's question. I opened my mouth to answer but closed it immediately. All I could do was shake my head slowly.

Keira giggled. "I don't remember either."

"Maybe we could borrow the café server's phone and call Yuan's convenience store?" I suggested. "Then we'd know our destination, and we can call a cab."

"Great plan," Keira agreed. "But you'd need to start screaming again to get the server's attention. She's disappeared again."

I crossed my arms defiantly, embarrassed and annoyed at the mention of my non-PG13 meltdown earlier. "Why don't *you* try it this time?"

"Can I confess something?"

I nodded.

Keira took a deep breath. "Earlier, I didn't come to the men's room to give you your bag or flashlight out of kindness in my heart." She paused for effect. "I came to tell you off before leaving this place on my own. When there was a power cut, I lost it. I blamed you for getting me into this whole mess, starting with convincing me to join the Mobile Rehab."

"Fair point."

"Wait, let me finish," Keira continued. "But when I saw the same frustration in you, I felt better and started looking at the brighter side. We could have been outside, cold and wet, stuck in the storm. Instead, we're lucky to be warm and dry in this cozy café."

"True."

She cleared her throat and spoke softly. "Thank you very much, Rory. It was really nice of you to accompany me tonight, even though you didn't have to."

"Thanks," I mumbled, avoiding looking at her.

Keira deserved more than a monosyllable response from me, but I was tongue-tied. Usually, when I went all quiet in a conversation, my chest would constrict, and I'd feel out of breath. But right now, I had an inexplicable warm and fuzzy feeling in my heart. It had been a long time since anyone had appreciated something I did, and it felt strange.

We awkwardly finished our coffee in silence as my mind drifted off to all the times I went out of my way to do something for someone with terrible consequences. I even got almost suspended from the university for no fault of mine.

The traumatic memory still sent a shudder down my spine, and I forced myself back to the present and focused on the warm glow of the candlelight on Keira's pretty face and hair as she grooved slowly to some invisible music. Her curls were like perfectly helical springs, that bounced gracefully every time she moved her head.

She closed her eyes as she savored her drink, softly tapping her long slender fingers on the cup as she lifted one of her hands to tuck the free, dancing strands of her hair behind her ear. I protested silently as she did that, but then I realized how creepy I looked staring at her like this.

I averted my eyes immediately to the plate of egg tarts, chuckling to myself, remembering how Keira thought they are poisoned.

Being stuck in the middle of nowhere amidst a storm sucked. But I was glad that, at the very least, I wasn't alone.

Chapter 6

Keira

I took my notebook out of my bag and placed it on the table, glad I hadn't lost my touch. I always got new song ideas when I least expected it. I had pretended to groove to invisible music to save myself from the embarrassment of facing Rory after my honest confession. His monosyllable response threw me off, but I knew it was unfair to expect more. At least he wasn't rude and didn't laugh.

Unlike most of the other people in my life. My mother and brother hated honest conversations. So did my friends. But I continued to speak my mind until Diego made fun of my emotions. My boyfriend—soon-to-be ex—said I was too sentimental and cheesy. So I stopped sharing my feelings.

However, if I hadn't been honest with Rory, my guilty conscience would have killed me.

I set aside my thoughts about everything else and focused on the tune I was humming in my mind. In my song book, I penned the lyrics with the tune. If I had my guitar, this would have been much easier.

After jotting down just the first stanza for now, from the corner of my eyes, I saw Rory was busy drawing the egg tarts in his notebook. Suddenly, he sneezed into his elbow, and the table shook when he hit his hand against it. Before I could say "bless you," the candle on our table tipped over, and it was dark again.

"Sorry," Rory said, only to sneeze again three more times.

"Are you okay?"

Rory nodded but sneezed again.

I could still make out the outline of his face because of the faint glow of the solar-powered streetlights outside.

"Have you caught a cold?" I asked.

He shook his head. "The sneezing started suddenly. I have no idea why."

I got up from my seat. "Let me see if I can get you another hot drink."

"Thanks, but you don't have to. I'm not cold."

I sat back down. "Okay, let me know if you need anything."

"I appreciate your offer, but it's too dark for you to move around. You might get hurt."

I laughed. "I'll take the flashlight." I added mischievously, "Or maybe this time, *I* should curse like a sailor in the dark and get the café owner to attend to us."

Rory chuckled. "Are you ever going to stop pulling my leg about that? For the record, I don't swear often. That, er, wasn't my best moment."

"Don't worry about it. Our situation sucks." I added hesitantly, "I was planning to say worse things earlier. And it wouldn't even have been to myself."

"I admit that it's my fault you're stuck in this situation."

"No, it's not," I replied. "Things could be worse, and I'm sorry I blamed you. We've already been over this earlier."

"Alright, let's change the subject. Were you writing a song earlier?"

I nodded. "I'm the songwriter for my band."

"That's really cool. I wish I could play the guitar. I tried learning to impress my crush in middle school but gave up when I realized she liked someone else."

I laughed.

"Do you play any instruments?" Rory asked.

"Yes, I play the guitar, the keyboard, and the drums. I'm not an expert drummer but can manage if needed."

"Wow!"

"How about you?" I asked. "Are you an artist?"

Rory chuckled and shook his head. "Not at all. I started drawing again yesterday after many years. I used to sketch and paint a lot during my free time, until middle school, but then I got too busy. Swimming practice and tournaments took over my high school and college life."

"So you are an athlete," I stated, glad my guess was right.

"Kind of. It's complicated."

I sighed. "I get what you mean by complicated. I'm in a similar situation."

I thought about how, with Diego and me splitting, our band would be affected. Even without our relationship playing a role, I'd been considering leaving recently. But I was always worried about how our other bandmates—Savio and Marina, and my twin brother, Sebastian—would react.

"Can I ask you a question?"

I was thankful Rory interrupted my pointless thoughts. "Sure."

"How are you so fluent in English? I had a teammate in high school who moved to Canada from Brazil, and he struggled with learning the language."

"We lived in the States for a few years when I was a child," I answered. "We had to go back to Brazil after that. I continued to read a lot of English novels to improve my language skills."

"That's cool. I hate reading."

I rolled my eyes. "Even though almost none of my friends read, I will never, ever understand that statement."

"It's so boring," Rory said. "When I open a novel, I fall asleep."

"Maybe you don't read the right books. What genres have you tried?"

Rory sighed. "All of them: thriller, mystery, fantasy, romance, nonfiction. None of them hold my attention. I do like audiobooks though."

I made a face. "Audiobooks aren't for me. My mind drifts away when I try listening to them. I couldn't even concentrate on my all-time favorite book, *Relentless* by Walter Lauren, for more than a few minutes."

"Oh. Walt is my best friend's dad!"

"Really?" I squealed like an excited kid. "You're joking, aren't you?"

Rory opened his backpack and fished out the yet-to-be released hardcover of the sequel of *Relentless, Incessant.* "See. He's signed here with a special note."

"'Son, I know you don't like to read, but I hope you enjoy this one. Love, Walt.'" I read the neat cursive handwriting aloud. "I'm so jealous."

"I really enjoyed listening to *Relentless,* but this physical book doesn't interest me at all. Walt's publishers aren't releasing the audiobook until later this year."

"Let me borrow it then," I said. "I've preordered the book and can't wait to start reading it."

"What do I get in return?" Rory teased.

"What do you want?"

He pointed to the plate on the table. "These tarts."

"Eat them. What's stopping you?"

"You," he replied. "Try a piece first. If you're okay, I'll eat them all."

I raised an eyebrow. "You know that, if anything happens to me, you'll be the first suspect, right?"

Rory laughed. "Fine. Forget the tarts. Get us back to our apartment before dawn, and the book is yours."

"Mine...as in?"

"As in, I'll give it to you," Rory clarified. "Not just let you borrow it."

"Deal."

I reluctantly got up from my seat with my flashlight. I felt too lazy to go and look for the café owner or any other means to get out of this place. All I wanted to do was sleep. And resting on the futons in our apartment sounded better than spending the entire night at this café. Besides, the pain in my ears was killing me right now, and I couldn't apply the drops unless I laid down.

I knocked on the kitchen door behind the cashier's desk a few times, hoping the server would come out. But no one did. I tried opening it, but it was locked. Annoyed, I searched for a landline with my flashlight.

The desk was nearly empty except for a computer, the card machine, and a pen stand. I went behind the table to check the keyboard drawer. This was just like the one at home where I'd left my mobile phone.

My mind drifted off to the last conversation I had had before I had angrily switched off the device and stashed it in my drawer. I wondered if anyone had tried to contact me. Probably not. After all, I had asked them not to.

Shaking off my thoughts, I flashed the light across the keyboard drawer. There it was, the telephone hiding behind the credit card machine. With a ray of hope in my heart, I picked up the receiver, but there was no ringtone.

I kneeled on the floor to ensure the device was connected properly to the port.

"What are you doing, ma'am?"

I jumped at the sudden voice, hitting my head against table.

"Sorry, I didn't mean to scare you," a woman I hadn't seen before said. She was drenched from head to toe. "Are you okay?"

"Are you hurt?" Rory asked at the same time.

"I'm alright," I replied. "I was trying to make the landline work."

"None of the phone lines are working because of the storm," the woman answered. She showed us her phone. "My mobile phone doesn't have network either. Do you need to call someone?"

"Do you know Yuan's convenience store?" I asked.

"I'm not sure," the lady answered. "Can you tell me the name of the store?"

"It's the one with the bright green sign board," Rory replied.

"There are many stores with a green board in this area," the woman said, drying her hair with a towel. "I'll quickly change into some dry clothes and come back to help you."

"She must be the owner," Rory said when the woman went in the back.

"What about the other lady who served us the coffee and egg tarts, then?" I asked.

Rory shrugged. "Maybe they're business partners."

"Possible."

"I'm back," the woman announced a few minutes later, tying on her apron with the café's logo. "First, let me apologize for our terrible service. My cook told me how you both waited for a long time before she could attend to you. She didn't know that no one else was in the café. She doesn't speak English. My server went out for a delivery two hours ago and hasn't come back yet. She must be stuck in the storm. And I stepped out for a quick errand but got delayed because it started pouring. I'm really sorry, again. Whatever you order tonight will be complimentary."

"That's alright," I said.

"We understand," Rory added.

"Thank you. So, how can I help you?"

For the next half an hour, Rory and I described our building and Yuan's convenience store in elaborate detail. But it wasn't enough to locate our "home" on the map. The café owner asked us questions about the shops we had seen on our bus ride, but we couldn't recall anything.

We were so used to sending our locations on our phone that we never felt the need to remember any landmarks when we went out.

Oh, how I missed having a mobile phone with internet. What did people use in the ancient days? I mean, before smartphones were invented.

Someone rang the bell at the entrance, and the owner left to attend to the new customers.

I turned toward Rory. "Why didn't we write down the name and address of the hotel in our building, knowing we'd have no internet connection?"

"We really *are* dependent on our phones and the internet for everything," Rory said. "It's become almost impossible to do anything without our devices."

I nodded. "True."

"That's why I find it hard to believe that you forgot yours before traveling to a different country."

My eyes widened, and my mouth went dry in panic. I prayed Rory didn't notice. I didn't want to reveal the real reason I didn't bring my phone.

"I can't believe it either," I replied, hoping Rory wouldn't ask any further questions.

"Well, we have to spend the night here. We don't really have a choice."

I thought about the soft futon at the apartment, wishing a magic spell would take me there. I sighed. "Yeah. It sucks."

Rory and I removed our shoes and put our feet up on the booth seat. We leaned against the wall to make ourselves a little more comfortable.

"Do you mind if I stretch my legs out for a bit?" Rory asked.

I shook my head. "Not at all. Your feet may dangle though. These booth seats are not long enough for you."

Rory sighed. "I hate being tall."

"People like tall partners though," I pointed out with a laugh. "In every romance book, the guy is tall."

Rory made a face. "Yeah, what's with that?"

The café owner got us some warm blankets. "I hope these help for now. I'll let you know when the internet is back, and we can search for your hotel online together. Maybe the photos will help you locate it. Let me know if you need more coffee."

"Thanks," Rory said. "But how can you make coffee when the power is out?"

"We use gas stoves," the owner replied. "They don't need electricity to run. Would you like more coffee?"

Rory shook his head. "Not for me. Keira?"

"Thanks, I'm good too."

When the owner left, I couldn't stop thinking about how our only solution was to wait for the internet to start working again. It was scary how dependent we were on technology and couldn't survive even for a few hours without it.

"Are you planning to take a nap?" Rory asked, interrupting my thoughts.

I sighed. "No. I can't fall asleep like this. How about you?"

"I'm about to fall off this seat, in case you haven't noticed. My, um, backside is too wide for this booth seat. And my feet are hanging, which worsens my balance. I'm the two-in-one Daddy Long Legs and Daddy Big Back!"

I giggled despite feeling bad for him. "Sorry. I'm not making fun of you. Your explanation is funny."

Rory laughed with me. "Jokes might be the only way to get through this endless night."

"Yes," I agreed. "And your company."

I mentally kicked myself for letting the last three words out of my mouth. Had I made Rory uncomfortable again? Why did I have to make things awkward all the time?

"Thanks, Keira." Rory spoke softly, looking me in the eyes, his expression sincere. "Tonight would have been worse without your company." He paused, placing both his feet back on the ground and sat upright. "And thank you for always speaking your mind. You really know how to say the right things. Though I'm not the best at responding to them."

Rory's words made me feel warm and fuzzy inside. It was nice to escape from my messy life by chatting and joking with him.

At least for the time being.

Chapter 7

Rory

Keira and I decided to write down all the things we could do to survive without our cell phones and the internet. Today's events had made us realize how unprepared we were for the nondigital life, and if we were to make it in this foreign land, we needed to pull up our socks.

"Write down the names and phone numbers of all the places we plan to visit," Keira said. "Let's start with the hotel in our building and Yuan's convenience store."

"Note down landmarks when we travel." I scribbled in my notebook. "And study the map thoroughly beforehand."

"Ensure our Octopus cards are topped up regularly," Keira added. "Carry enough cash with us. But not too much. We don't want to get robbed."

I included that and closed my notebook. "That should do for now."

Keira nodded. "Good job. We will not get lost again in Hong Kong."

I laughed. "Are you being sarcastic?"

"Obviously. I bet anything we're going to run into more such wacky situations."

As if in response to her words, the café door opened, and someone barged inside. What now?

"Rory, Keira, oh thank goodness you both are okay."

Keira and I sprang up from our seats, delighted to see Desmond and Champa. We hugged them. They were drenched from head to toe.

Had they searched for us the entire night? Had they walked from the apartment all the way? How did they manage to find us? I had so many questions I wanted to ask, but I was too moved to utter a single word.

"Get something warm to drink," Keira told them. "You must be cold."

"There's no time for that," Champa replied. "Yuan and Grandpa Yu are waiting in the car for us. We need to hurry."

Keira and I went to find the café owner to let her know we were leaving. She refused to let us pay for the coffee and the sweets, insisting they was complimentary. We thanked her for her thoughtfulness and promised her we would come back.

When we went back to the table to clean up, we saw Desmond and Champa stuffing their faces with the egg tarts.

"Why didn't you eat these?" Desmond asked with his mouth full. "They're delicious."

Keira and I looked at each other at the same time and shared a secret smile. Our private joke would stay between us.

"We weren't hungry," I said.

"We planned to bring them home for you guys," Keira added.

"We saved you one each," Champa said, placing the tarts on a paper napkin and handing them to us.

I took a bite of the crispy outer shell, enjoying the feel of the sweet creamy filling coat my mouth. I would never forget these egg tarts from this café—neither their taste, nor the feeling of sharing them with friends who had been mere strangers until a few hours ago.

I wouldn't forget the two people who saved us from the distress of spending the night in a café booth.

And I would definitely remember my weird partner in crime and her ridiculous theories—the only one who had ever been able stop me from touching a sweet treat!

***

We ran to the car, which was parked right outside the café. The vehicle looked old, due to the paint peeling off in many places. Desmond struggled to open the passenger back door. I tried to help him, but it was stuck. Champa tugged at it once and opened it. But the door hit her in the face.

"Are you okay?" all of us asked in unison.

Grandpa Yu got down from the car, concerned. "Ensure you ice your nose tonight. It'll swell badly, otherwise."

Champa nodded. "I'm fine, thanks."

I wondered why Grandpa Yu had come to pick us up when Yuan was the one driving. There was space for only five people in the car. And we were six. Now, the four of us would have to squeeze in together in this tiny backseat. And fitting in small areas was not my forte.

Keira nudged me. "Get in first. The rest of us will adjust."

I slid to the far end of the seat, followed by Desmond in the middle. Keira got in next, and Champa sat on her lap reluctantly.

"You would have never got back home today without me," Grandpa Yu started. "I guessed that both of you would have taken the wrong bus when Yuan and your friends told me what happened. I used my brains to find out which bus. It was very easy, but none of you kids would have figured it out."

"Grandpa guessed correctly that you took Bus 14B instead of 14, which is why you ended up here," Yuan explained.

Grandpa Yu went on. "People your age lack common sense and life skills. You're all too dependent on technology."

Though I was too tired to admit it aloud, Grandpa Yu was right. We *were* too pampered by our cell phones and the internet. But I wished he wasn't so hard on us.

"Didn't Grandpa Yu go home earlier?" I asked in a low tone.

"He was there when we went looking for you," Desmond said. "He heard us talking to Yuan."

"What if the internet connection doesn't ever come back?" Grandpa Yu continued. "What will you all do then?"

"Don't say that, Grandpa," Yuan replied. "I need to finish my paper for school."

Grandpa Yu scoffed. "You don't need the internet to do your homework. You can go to the library and use books. You people have everything at your fingertips. That's what's spoiling you." He turned and pointed at me. "Do you know the name of our convenience store?"

"Er, Yu's Convenience store?" I asked sheepishly, knowing I was wrong.

Grandpa Yu shook his head. "How about Champa and Desmond? You've been there more than once today."

"It's the one with the green board," Desmond answered.

Champa simply shook her head.

I looked at Keira, who shrugged, with a bored expression on her face.

"See, none of you know." Grandpa Yu handed us a flyer with the store's name. "Learn it now." He shook his head and continued mocking us. "Your generation does not know the value of anything. That's because you all have it too easy. You don't know what it means to struggle. Look at me, for example. I still live without a mobile phone. And I have traveled across the world. I've lived in more than four countries. I speak five languages. I have made a lot of money. Mind you, I started out with only a hundred dollars in my pocket at your age. Hong Kong dollars. Do you know how difficult that is? When I went to the Philippines, I had to toil day and night. Not like you, who have everything handed to you on a platter."

I tuned out Grandpa Yu, who continued to ramble about himself. My eyes met Yuan's in the rearview mirror. He mouthed an embarrassed "sorry." Desmond and Champa were trying hard not to laugh. And Keira was fast asleep. I wondered if it was better when Grandpa Yu interfered in others' lives or talked about himself.

I nodded off before I could think about it further.

***

When I woke up, I wondered where I was. The mattress underneath my body was soft, and the cotton blanket covering me was warm. I tried to open my eyes wider, but the sun was too bright. I looked at my watch groggily. It was noon.

Desmond was fast asleep on the futon adjacent to mine, on the "other side" of the room. The area was so small that there was only about three inches of space between our futons. Desmond had squished his back to the wall to give me a little more privacy.

Last night, when Yuan dropped us off, Desmond had guided the rest of us sleepy-heads up to the apartment. I only remembered plopping onto the already-made bed.

I got up from my bed and freshened up in the bathroom. When I went to make breakfast, Keira was in the kitchen beating eggs in a bowl, deep in thought about something.

"Good morning," I greeted her.

"Morning, Rory. Did you sleep well?"

I nodded. "Like a baby. And you?"

She shrugged. "A little bit."

"Why? Did you have ear pain?"

"Yes, I woke up because of the pain," Keira replied. "But applying the ear drops helped."

"I'm glad."

"Can I pick your brain about something?" Keira asked.

"Sure."

She took a deep breath. "So, this is about a friend. She is in a band with four other people—her boyfriend, her guy best friend, her brother, and her girl best friend. Her girl best friend is also her brother's girlfriend. Now, her boyfriend is cheating on her with someone else. And her guy best friend confessed his feelings for her. What do you think my friend should do?"

Keira looked at me eagerly as I thought about her question. I needed a moment to let it sink in. The whole situation seemed confusing. If I were in Keira's "friend's" place, I would run away from this mess. But I didn't want to be insensitive to Keira's feelings. I guessed the "friend" in this story was actually her.

"Does your friend like her guy best friend too?" I asked.

"She used to," Keira replied. "But that was long ago, and he didn't feel the same way back then."

"How is your friend holding up? Being cheated on must make her feel terrible."

Keira looked sad for a moment but composed herself immediately. "She's fine. But I feel angry about her situation. Just imagine how she must have felt when she saw her boyfriend of three years kiss someone else. And can you believe the nerve of her guy best friend, who decided to confess his feelings *right then*?"

"He shouldn't have made it all about him. His timing was wrong."

"Exactly," Keira exclaimed. "See, you get it. Why can't my friends understand? How is any of this my fault?"

I didn't want to point out to Keira that she had forgotten she was talking about her "friend." I admired how she could talk about what was bothering her, albeit indirectly. A lot of things were on *my* mind, but I chose not to think about them. If I pretended they didn't exist, they would go away. Fake it till you make it, right?

"It's not your friend's fault at all," I said, shifting my focus back to Keira. "Since you asked what I think your friend should do, I'll say this. She must focus on her own needs and happiness. It's sad her friends don't understand her, but she mustn't concern herself with that right now."

Keira grinned widely. "Thanks. I'll let her know that." She added after a pause, "You can talk about your 'friend's' problems with me too. I'll be happy to listen to you without any judgment."

I smiled. "Thanks. I'll remember your offer in the future." I pointed to the eggs she was stirring. "Now, what's cooking? I'm starving."

"I decided to make breakfast for everyone this morning," Keira replied. "Champa and Desmond did a lot in our absence yesterday. They labeled the meat pans, so my vegetarian food stays separate. They placed the bread and other snack packets on a plate filled with water like a moat to protect the food from the ants they noticed last night. And they made our beds."

"The least we can do is make lunch for them," I said.

"I'll make scrambled eggs and grill the tofu. Can you cook the breakfast meats for you and Desmond?"

"Sure," I replied. "But wait, who stocked the refrigerator? It was empty last night."

"Desmond and Champa must have bought stuff from Yu Hoi Pou when they went looking for us last night."

"Yes, they got frozen veggies too," I said opening the freezer and showing me the vegetable packets. "And...we finally learned the name of Yuan's store."

Within the next fifteen minutes, we got everything ready for break-fast sandwiches. Keira slathered a generous amount of catupiry cheese and hot sauce on four slices of bread.

"You don't have your phone, but you have these condiments?" I teased.

Keira laughed. "I can't survive without my cheese or hot sauce." She showed me a jar labeled "Champa's special spice mix." "See, Champa also thinks like me."

I spooned up some spice powder and tasted it. "Yum. This is amaz-ing. Let's use this for our dish."

I took some frozen veggies in a bowl and blanched them. I seasoned them with salt, pepper, and the fragrant garlic-based spice mix Cham-pa had brought from home.

"Who's making yummy food?" Desmond asked from across the room. "Or am I dreaming?"

"Food will be served in five minutes," Keira called out.

Desmond came running. "Are you serious?"

Keira and I chuckled at his childlike enthusiasm. "Yes."

"Champs, wake up, sleepyhead," he said. "You don't want to miss this amazing hot meal custom-made for us."

Champa looked up from her futon reluctantly. "I don't want to get out of bed. Let me sleep. It's still too early in the morning."

"It's almost one in the afternoon," Desmond replied. "Can you believe we haven't eaten anything in over fifteen hours?"

Champa rolled her eyes at him, pushing herself upright. "Fine. Give me five minutes."

Within five minutes, the four of us sat on the folded-up futons—which looked like couches—with our plates. We ate our yummy, loaded breakfast sandwiches, chatting about the ingredients and our favorite foods.

After our meal, we took turns washing the dishes and cleaning the kitchen. Though we had had only two meals together, I felt like I had known the other three forever. We talked and laughed as we did the chores.

Then the four of us sat in the living room with our notebooks open.

"Alright, so let's plan our time here," Desmond said. "We need to set our budget and decide the places to visit. We must also assign tasks for everyone fairly."

"Des, I'll fix the mosquito mesh in your room window," Champa volunteered. "You said you feel claustrophobic in there."

"I'll plan budget meals for us," Keira said. "We can have a mix of takeout and home-cooked food in the apartment. And when we go out, I'll help us get cheap food."

"And I'll assign tasks for everyone," Desmond said. "We'll do our own laundry and wash our respective plates and cutlery. But we'll share other chores on rotation."

"And I will do whatever you all say," I declared. "I'll follow the bosses."

Everyone looked at me, confused. There was an awkward silence in the room.

"Sorry, did I seem too authoritative?" Desmond asked.

I shook my head. "Of course not."

"Then why would you do whatever we say?" Keira asked.

I could feel sweat trickling down my forehead onto my eyebrow as everyone looked at me, expecting an answer. My chest constricted as I felt a panic attack building up. I hated being confronted by anyone. It reminded me of someone I wanted to forget.

I was happy to listen to others, because I knew I would always make the wrong decision.

I hadn't done anything right recently, and I blamed myself for it.

My best friend got hurt...because of me.

My family was upset...because of me.

And I was miserable...because of me.

I excused myself before anyone could tell something was up. I didn't want anyone to know my terrible secret, which I'd hidden from my family and friends for so long.

I ran to the bathroom, fumbling in my pockets for my phone. I desperately needed a distraction now before the unwanted thoughts flooded my mind. But there was nothing in my pocket except my retracting pen. I plopped on the closed toilet seat and closed my eyes, pressing the back of my pen as fast as I could. I focused on the clicking sound to calm down.

After a few minutes, I felt better and went back to the others as if nothing had happened.

"Sorry, I had to use the restroom urgently," I said. "I was joking earlier. I'll look up economical places for us to visit and draft an itinerary. How about each of you give me your lists? I'll compile them."

Desmond gave me a sheet of paper. "Cool, here's Champa's and mine."

Keira pulled her chair closer to mine and examined Desmond's list. She scribbled more names on the list. "I would like to add these places, too, please."

I nodded. "Give me an hour, and I'll be ready with the itinerary."

"Um, actually, can we go to the Ten Thousand Buddhas Monastery right now?" Desmond asked. "I checked the map and the brochure, and it's close by. We need to get off at the next metro station and walk for ten minutes."

"I'm game if everyone else is," I said.

"We should get duplicate keys in case we want to travel separately," Champa stated.

"I'll ask the hotel reception downstairs where we can find a locksmith when we're back from the monastery," Keira said.

"Or we could ask Yuan," Desmond suggested. "He gave us his old mobile device for emergencies. It's not a smartphone, but we could try calling him if we need to."

My eyes lit up. "Did we get a mobile phone? That's awesome. We don't have to worry about the Mobile Rehab rules anymore. Let's switch it on."

"Who'll pay for the calls?" Keira asked.

"We will," Champa answered. "Yuan told us it's Grandpa Yu's, but he's never used it."

We tried to switch on the device, but it didn't work.

"Maybe it's out of battery," I said. "Let's try charging it."

"I charged it last night," Desmond replied. "For the *entire* night."

"How about we try pressing the power button really hard?" Keira suggested.

Champa pressed the power button for a long time, and the device switched on. All of us clapped and cheered gleefully.

But our happiness was short-lived when the phone switched off again within a few seconds.

"Maybe this is a sign that we should try to stay without our phones for the rest of the trip," Keira said.

I nodded reluctantly. "Yeah. You're right."

"Yuan offered to give us his friend's old smartphone, but we refused," Champa said.

Desmond pointed to the tiny analog alarm clock he'd bought last night. "We need to leave now if we want to see the monastery before closing time."

"Are you really going to carry that clock in your pocket?" Champa asked, sounding amused. "You should have just got a watch instead."

"You know I don't wear watches," Desmond replied. "Besides, this is temporary. I can't wait to carry my cell phone again."

We walked to the nearest metro station, which was only a few minutes away from our place. Our train arrived immediately.

"Guys, if one of us gets separated from the group, the others should wait near the station exit," I said when we entered the metro. "Let's try not to lose each other."

"Agreed," everyone else replied in unison.

Within seconds, our compartment was full, and the four of us were almost standing on top of each other. We wore our backpacks in the front to prevent theft, which made it more uncomfortable. But before we could try to shift positions, we reached our stop. The metro was super fast.

We managed to exit the station together and walked to the Ten Thousand Buddhas Monastery. It was already three, and I wondered why Desmond wanted to visit a place that would close in two hours. Besides, we had to climb about 450 steps to reach our destination.

As we climbed, I was mesmerized by the number of gold-colored Buddha statues adjacent to every stair. The brochure mentioned that there were a total of 13,000 idols in the monastery area, and every one of them was different. I would have loved to take my time and look at each of these structures, but Desmond and Champa seemed to be in a hurry. They ran up the stairs as if their lives depended on it.

Keira stood on the first step and looked around in a leisurely manner with a smile. She seemed to share an intimate moment with the surroundings, and I didn't want to disturb her.

I took my camera from my bag and snapped pictures of the statues, the stairs, and the pagoda on top of the hill. I wore the camera around my neck and climbed slowly, enjoying the afternoon breeze on my face. It was quiet and calm, except for the sounds of birds chirping. I could hear my own breath loud and clear.

Suddenly, I felt my breathing pace quicken out of nowhere. My heart palpitated against my chest, and I started gasping for air. I tried to run up the stairs as fast as I could, not wanting Keira to notice my panic attack. But I could only climb a couple of steps. Thankfully, I was near a landing that had a bench.

When I felt like I couldn't move anymore, I sat down and hyperventilated. Thankfully, no one was close by to see me in this pitiful state.

I took deeper, slower breaths to calm myself down, like I had read online when these had started—after my best friend stopped talking to me suddenly without any explanation.

All because of *her*.

I tried to think happy thoughts, but *her* voice kept ringing in my ears.

"You are pathetic, Rory Matthews. You are overreacting as usual."

She had been right.

I was overreacting.

Everything was fine.

I was fine.

What was not fine was this stupid panic attack that came out of nowhere, for no reason.

And it had nothing to do with me.

CHAPTER 8

Keira

I watched Rory, clearly having a panic attack, from a distance. I didn't want to approach him and make him feel uneasy. However, I didn't want to leave him alone either. I'd had panic attacks before, and I knew how embarrassing they were. The last thing I'd wanted was for someone to see *me* in that state.

I pretended to examine one of the statues as I waited for Rory to calm down. When he slowly started climbing up the stairs again, I ran toward him.

"Hey, Rory, do you mind taking my photo with this scenic background?"

Rory smiled brightly, trying his best to look fine. "Sure. With your camera?"

I nodded and gave him my Polaroid.

He clicked a picture that printed instantly. It looked great. I invited him to take a selfie with me and took two, so I could give him a copy of the printed photograph.

"Wow, your Polaroid is handy," Rory exclaimed.

"Yes, but I can't take too many pictures. The film can be hard to find."

"Save your pictures for later then," Rory said. "Use mine. I'll email you the photographs later."

"Thanks."

We climbed the stairs in comfortable silence until I spotted a group of monkeys approaching us.

I nudged Rory. "Keep your camera in your backpack. I'll do the same. We don't want these monkeys taking our stuff."

We placed our cameras inside our backpacks and walked up casually, ignoring the monkeys. But one of them screeched so loudly that both of rushed up the stairs as fast as we could. I knew it wasn't wise to run from wild animals. They would smell our fear and chase us. Besides, there was no way we could outrun these monkeys.

However, logic and rules took a backseat as fear took over. We ran and didn't stop until we reached the pagoda at the top. Thankfully, the monkeys had stopped following us.

When we finally caught our breath, I noticed Rory's hand was holding mine. We let go of each other immediately, and I felt the blood rushing to my face. I wasn't sure whether it was because of the warmth of his touch or our run. From the corner of my eye, I saw Rory trying to hide his pink-tinged face.

"I can't believe we climbed 400 stairs in less than ten minutes," I said, trying to break the awkward silence. "Thanks to those monkeys."

"We definitely broke a speed record today," Rory replied with a chuckle.

Before we knew it, both of us were clutching our stomachs and laughing, recalling how we ran from the monkeys. It was funny now, but a few minutes back, my heart had been in my mouth at the thought of being attacked by the unpredictable animals.

We stopped when one of the tourists glared at us and placed a finger to their lips. I mouthed a *sorry* and felt terrible for being noisy in this serene, sacred environment.

We were surrounded by more Buddha statues in the vast corridor. In front of us was the main entrance to the monastery, a beautiful red building embossed with golden dragons on both sides. We didn't get a chance to go inside because we were too late. It was almost closing time.

We strolled and enjoyed the sights of the other magnificent structures in the vicinity. There was a nine-floor pagoda, also red in color, decorated with bells and more golden statues at every level. The brilliant red and gold color combination was pleasing and calming.

"There is a lot to see here," Rory stated. "We'd need at least three hours to see all these pavilions and read about them."

I nodded. "And there is a vegetarian restaurant on the premises with sattvic food. I would have loved to try their unique dishes without onion or garlic."

"I wonder why Desmond wanted to come here so close to closing time?"

I had overheard Desmond and Champa talking about searching for someone here, but I didn't say anything to Rory. It wasn't my business, and I didn't want to gossip.

"Maybe we can come back here sometime next week," I suggested.

"That's a great idea."

"Are we waiting here for Champa and Desmond?" I asked. "Or should we go downstairs? This place will close soon."

"Let's wait for them downstairs," Rory answered. "But first, let's take the banana from that gentleman calling us." He gestured toward a man offering everyone a banana.

I took the fruit from him, even though I didn't want it. It felt rude to decline.

"Eat them right away," the gentleman told us. "The monkeys might—"

Two monkeys raced by, jumping up and snatching the fruits from Rory's and my hands. We were mortified. Another one grabbed the entire bunch from the gentleman, who screamed in fear. Before we knew it, the naughty animals had peeled the bananas and hurled the peels at us, running up a tall tree to enjoy their treats.

The gentleman shouted at the monkeys in Cantonese, but the monkeys mocked him by making faces. The situation was hilarious and embarrassing in equal measures. Rory and I bit back our laughter, because the gentleman looked traumatized by the incident. We didn't want to be impolite. People had gathered around us at the commotion. They tried to console the poor man. We thanked the gentleman for the fruit and excused ourselves.

On our way down the stairs, and when we were far away from the man, Rory and I burst into laughter.

"I can't believe how everything happened within a flash of a second," Rory said. "The monkeys were so fast!"

"It was unbelievable. I don't think we'll ever forget this incident."

Rory nodded. "This is just like the time when my parents, sister, and I went camping one summer. We set up our tents in the afternoon, and I went to use the restroom. When I came out to wash my hands, I felt someone poke my back. Thinking it was my mischievous sister, I pushed without checking who it was. When my hands touched fur instead of human skin, I turned, realizing I was face to face with an old moose cow. I was too flummoxed to scream and ran as fast as possible back to the camp."

"Oh my goodness. That must have been terrifying."

Rory chuckled. "I still wonder if I imagined the moose and thanked my stars she was old. Otherwise, there was a good chance she'd have attacked me. When we went back, the animal had disappeared."

I laughed. "She came to say hello to you privately."

"Yes, I think so too. Riley still teases me about that day."

"That sounds exactly like my brother, Sebastian," I said. "If siblings find something to make fun of us about, they don't let go until they have something new."

"Yes, exactly. Look at what my sister did to me."

Rory opened his backpack and took out a silver device with earphones. I had seen the music player before, because my dad had one, but couldn't remember what it was called. Rory handed me one of the earbuds and gestured for me to place it in my ear. He pressed the play button and asked me to wait for the music.

I was confused until I heard the following words. "Our digestive system starts with our mouth and ends with our anus. When we eat, our teeth and our saliva cut down the food particles into smaller pieces. Saliva is secreted from salivary glands contains salivary amylase."

I giggled. "Don't tell me that's your sister's voice."

Rory made a face. "Who else would do that to me?"

I looked at the tape case in Rory's hands. It was that of an old band from twenty years ago.

"Did she record over the original music?"

Rory nodded.

"That's a brilliant prank," I exclaimed. When Rory scowled at me, I added, "It was so *mean* of her. She shouldn't have done that."

"It's okay, you can laugh," Rory said, cracking a grin. "I will admit that it was funny when people at the airport thought I was listening to some legendary music instead of my sister droning on about the digestive system. I even head-banged to her monotonous voice."

I snorted in laughter, imagining Rory grooving to his sister's textbook narration. "I wish I'd been there to witness it."

Rory continued telling me about his adventures at the airport. It was hysterical how a social media influencer had tried to interview him. Suddenly, mid-story, Rory lost his balance on the steps. He stopped himself from falling, but I knew this was an aftermath of the panic attack. I also used to feel dizzy after hyperventilating.

"Are you okay?" I asked, offering him my water bottle.

Rory nodded and took a sip of water from his own bottle. "Yes. It's just this heat. I'm not used to it."

It was a sunny but pleasant evening. It wasn't hot at all, but I didn't point this out to Rory. I wondered what bothered him so much. He always seemed so cheerful. What was he hiding underneath the façade of his carefree attitude?

"Do you want to get an ice lolly?" I asked. "I'm craving something sweet and fruity."

Ice lollies or juice always helped me gain energy after hyperventilating.

"Sure. We can get some while we wait downstairs." He ran down the rest of the stairs. "Let's race. The loser pays for the winner's treat."

"Hey, not fair," I protested. "We should have started the race together. You're cheating."

Rory laughed as he scurried down the stairs and I followed him. I didn't go down too fast and only pretended to race him. We were near the bottom, past all the steep steps. So, it was safe for us to race.

I paid for two orange Popsicles and handed one of them to Rory. "I'm going to get you for this unfair race."

Rory snickered. "Challenge accepted."

We enjoyed our sweet treats in silence near the exit gate, waiting for Desmond and Champa. My mind drifted back to the time when my father told me stories about his visit to this monastery with his friends. He used to show me photographs of this place with a twinkle in his eyes as he fondly remembered the "good old days." Now, I had sweet memories of my own, and it felt like he was present with me at this moment. I smiled and whispered secretly to him, "Thank you for bringing me here and making me a part of your favorite memories, Pai."

"Hey, Keira," Rory called out to me softly. "Thanks a lot for everything today. I wasn't feeling good earlier, but I really enjoyed this afternoon because of you."

"You're welcome. I had a fantastic time with you too."

Rory and I stood there, just looking at each other with matching shy smiles on our faces. My heart was racing, and I wondered if his was too.

And I wished we could stay this way for a while longer.

Just a little longer.

CHAPTER 9

Rory

My heart thumped loudly in my chest as I looked at Keira. Her smile was reassuring and comforting. I felt like I could open up a little more to her, the way she had done with me.

I cleared my throat. "Uh, you told me I could talk about my friend…"

Suddenly, Desmond and Champa came running toward us. Their timing was so bad! Couldn't they have come a few minutes later?

"Rory, Keira. There you are," Desmond said. "Sorry we disappeared like that."

Champa lifted a bag and waved it gently in front of us. "Look, we got free food."

"Yay," Keira and I replied in unison, the disappointment of being interrupted evident in our voices. I hoped we sounded more enthusiastic than we looked. But they seemed too excited to notice.

"How did you get free food?" Keira asked, as we walked together toward the metro station.

"I was the lucky hundredth person to enter the vegetarian restaurant inside the monastery," Champa responded.

"They had prizes for the fiftieth and the hundredth customers. I won their special meal for four."

"Cool," I replied. "Tonight's dinner is sorted then."

"Should we get duplicate keys before going back to the apartment?" Desmond asked.

"That's a good idea," Keira said. "We can inquire at the information desk."

The customer service representative at the metro station's information desk gave us some locksmiths' phone numbers. We jotted them down but didn't know how to call them. The landline in our apartment didn't work, and there were too many people in line behind us to request the representative let us use their phone.

"My mother told me they used public payphones before cell phones were invented," Keira said. "Have you seen any, by any chance?"

I asked one of the people waiting in line if there was a payphone in the metro station. They told me that the nearest one was a few stops away and that it was on a different route. We would need to change trains to get there.

We agreed it was too much of a hassle to go through all this for a few phone calls. Besides, none of us had coins for a payphone.

As we talked, I felt like someone was staring at us. When I turned around to check who it was, there was no one. I figured I'd imagined it and continued our discussion.

We walked toward the train, and the notion that someone was following us came back. I tried to make eye contact with Keira to see if she'd noticed.

Our eyes met and she mouthed, *Who is that?*

I shook my head slightly and shrugged.

Desmond and Champa seemed oblivious to the situation, and I felt it was best to stay quiet about it for now. I didn't want us to panic about something that was probably nothing.

When we got on the train, Keira leaned close to my ear. "That guy got onto the train too."

I gasped. "Did you see him?"

She nodded.

"Should we inform Desmond and Champa?"

Keira shook her head. "Let's keep this between us for now."

I agreed.

When we got off the train, Keira stood on the platform, trying to find the man. She drank water from her bottle so as not to make it obvious that she was looking for someone.

I walked toward her. "Did you see his face?" I asked.

Keira shook her head. "It was hidden. He was wearing a black cap, a black jacket, and olive-green pants. For a brief second, I thought I saw a mustache. But I'm not sure."

A shudder went down my spine. Criminals covered their faces. Who was this guy and why was he following us?

"Let's go," Keira whispered. "He must not suspect us of noticing him. If he knows we're onto him, it's even more dangerous."

I left first and Keira followed me.

Desmond and Champa were waiting for us at the entrance of the metro station.

"Don't get scared, but someone was following us," Champa said.

"We noticed," I replied quietly. "Is he still?"

"He went in the other direction," Desmond said.

None of us talked during our walk back to the apartment. All of us were shaken by the scary incident.

I made a mental note to learn the Hong Kong emergency phone numbers by heart.

Who knew what else was in store for us during this trip?

***

We were ravenous when we reached home. Keira and I reheated the food as Desmond and Champa got the plates ready. We served ourselves and sat on the futon "couches" with our plates.

"Try the bean curd roll," Desmond said, taking a bite of the appetizer. "I bought four extra servings, one each. I figured they'd be good, because everyone in the restaurant seemed to be ordering them. The dinner combo had only two pieces per person."

"These are delicious," I replied. "Next time we go out, I'll treat you to whatever you want."

"Is it easier to use chopsticks?" Keira asked, pointing toward Desmond and me. "My roll is falling apart when I use my fingers."

"Here, let me show you." Champa demonstrated the technique to hold chopsticks. "Correct. Now you just pick up the roll like that."

"Wow, Keira, you got that right the first time," Desmond exclaimed. "Champa took forever to learn."

Champa gave him a playful shove. "That's because you're not a good teacher like me."

"Oh no, you're a horrible teacher," Desmond replied. "Who shouts at me while teaching me math?"

Champa ignored him and pointed to Keira. "That's perfect. You're a quick learner."

Keira beamed at the compliment. "Thanks. I've always wanted to learn to use chopsticks but never got a chance."

"And how did you learn, Rory?" Desmond asked me.

"My best friend is half Bhutanese," I replied. "We grew up together, so I've known how to use them practically since I was a toddler."

We enjoyed the bean curd rolls in silence, savoring their unique taste. The juicy umami filling was made of mushrooms, black fungus, water chestnuts, and carrots sautéed with sweet soy sauce and fresh ginger. This complemented the crunchy bean curd perfectly, making our tastebuds crave more. Within minutes, we had finished all the appetizers. At least for the moment, it took our minds off the mysterious person who had followed us.

The other dishes in the dinner combo were also tasty, although not showstoppers like the rolls. There was rice with veggies, saucy noodles, and fortune cookies. We finished everything and cleaned up.

After dinner, we did our chores and got to work on our respective tasks. It was hard to write without a table, but we didn't have a choice. I referred to the travel brochure and the map to create a budget-friendly itinerary for the next few days. Keira worked on our meal plans. Desmond created a timetable and assigned tasks for all of us. He also developed a budget for all non-food-related expenses. Champa went to the store to get the materials to repair the damaged mesh in the bedroom window.

When we finished our work and decided to help Champa, she had dismantled the window in the guys' room to remove the damaged mosquito mesh. We stood at the room's entrance and watched in awe as she expertly, single-handedly, fixed the new mosquito mesh and reinstalled the window. She was careful not to disturb the spider web near one of the corners of the window.

"Kill any mosquitoes that may have entered when I was working now, okay, Spidey?" She spoke to the spider in a gentle tone. "I'm sorry if I hurt your web because of my clumsiness. I hope you forgive me."

"That's my best friend," Desmond claimed softly, but proudly. "She cares about every creature in the world."

"She's really amazing," Keira and I agreed in unison.

"Where did she get those tools from?" I wondered loudly.

"Hey, Champs, where did you get the work gloves and tools?" Desmond asked.

Champa jumped, startled when she finally noticed us. "Goodness, you almost gave me a heart attack. Sorry, I didn't see you guys earlier."

"All good," I replied with a chuckle. "We were just admiring your work."

"I borrowed this stuff from the hotel downstairs." She removed her work gloves. "Okay, it's all done now. You guys can sleep peacefully tonight."

"Thanks, Champs," Desmond said, high-fiving her. "You're the best."

The four of us went back to our living room and discussed our respective plans. Everyone agreed on almost everything the others had developed. It was nice to stay with such easygoing people, who didn't make a fuss. These three were just like my friends back home. And so unlike *her*.

Wait, why did she come to my mind all of a sudden? I wanted to forget her existence. She was the root cause of all my problems. I'd been successful not thinking about her all day. Why did she haunt my mind now?

"It's just eight," Desmond said, pointing to his pocket-sized clock. "It's too early to sleep. How about we have a home spa?"

Keira frowned. "What do you mean by a home spa?"

"Desmond's hobby is to create chemical-free self-care products," Champa explained. "We can lounge together with his face masks, foot creams, and hand lotions."

"I've been wanting to ask you what you use to keep them so soft since I shook your hand yesterday," I blurted to Desmond.

He chuckled. "I love it when someone compliments me for that."

"Don't praise him too much though," Champa warned. "You'll regret it. He won't stop talking about his creations."

"Hey, I'm not that bad," Desmond protested, throwing his pen at Champa playfully.

She ducked, and it hit Keira instead.

"Sorry," Champa said. "Are you okay?"

Keira nodded but did not smile. "I'm fine, thanks."

"Keira, as a token of my apology, I'll give you one of my most famous face mask kits," Desmond declared.

Keira frowned. "I don't need it. Please excuse me. I need to use the bathroom."

I watched, perplexed as Keira left in a huff. I wondered why she looked so distressed.

"Des, not everyone is interested in self-care products," Champa chided.

Desmond sighed. "I was only trying to make up for accidentally throwing my pen at her. I didn't mean to annoy her."

Champa squeezed Desmond's hand reassuringly. "It's alright. When Keira's back, we'll ensure she's comfortable and doesn't feel compelled to do anything she doesn't want. More than anything, we both know how that feels."

"Champa's right," I said. "When Keira sees we're not forcing her, she may join us."

"Alright, then," Desmond replied. "I'll go get everything ready."

Champa got up too. "I'll help you."

When they had gone into the bedroom, I stared at the closed bathroom door and hoped Keira was okay. I contemplated asking if she was alright but decided against it.

Keira had silently supported me when I was in distress earlier today. Now it was my turn to return the favor.

CHAPTER 10

Keira

In the bathroom, I cussed silently at myself for the umpteenth time for embarrassing myself like that. It was really sweet of Desmond to offer me the self-care product he made, but it was too late to tell him that. I had gotten worked up for no apparent reason and walked away rudely.

I sighed, expecting the other three to say bad things about me behind my back like my friends always did. Whenever I expressed my dislike for beauty products, my friends and relatives dissed me. They said I fell short compared to my good-looking brother who'd inherited the genes from our father.

Though it hurt, I had learned to ignore everyone else, but there was one person's words I could not forget—my mother's.

"You're AMZ Beauty Care's CEO's daughter, Keira. You need to live up to that title. If you don't clean yourself up, how will you do that? Do you think Diego, or any other man would ever want you? It'll be your fault if your boyfriend leaves you. I wasn't blessed in the looks department, either, but I got work done on my face and body when I was your age, and voilà, I was called 'dazzling' and 'gorgeous.' Why can't you be like me?"

I clenched my fists, trying to tune out my mother's voice in my mind. I didn't want her to cloud my thoughts and make me cry right now. I wouldn't be able to hide my red eyes and puffy face from the others if I did.

I heard Desmond's voice from our living room. "I was only trying to make up for accidentally throwing my pen at her. I didn't mean to annoy her."

Oh no, I felt worse now for being unnecessarily rude to him.

"It's alright. When Keira's back, we'll ensure she's comfortable and doesn't feel compelled to do anything she doesn't want. More than anything, we both know how that feels," Champa replied.

Aww, they really cared about me.

"Champa's right," Rory said. "When Keira sees we're not forcing her, she may join us."

Hearing them, I couldn't stop my tears any longer. My new friends were so empathetic. Why couldn't my loved ones back home be like them? I knew the answer to that question. But it only made me sadder.

After a good cry and washing my face, I unlocked the bathroom door and went back to the living room, feeling more courageous about facing them. They'd accepted my discomfort without any judgment.

I opened my suitcase and took out three boxes labeled "AMZ Beauty Care." I'd brought these with me to sell, in case I ran short of money. The products were all the rage on social media, though I didn't care much for them.

I sat down with the three of them, who had applied a green-colored substance to their faces. Now, they were rubbing some cream on their feet.

"Hey, Keira," Desmond said. "I'm sorry about earlier."

I shook my head. "No, *I'm* sorry. I was rude. As a token of my apology, I got you all these."

Desmond grabbed one of the boxes and squealed gleefully. "OMG, I've heard so much about this brand. I'd be lying if I said my products aren't inspired by AMZ's social media videos."

"My mother's the CEO," I said. "I can send you more whenever you want."

"You're giving us all this for *free*?" Rory asked. "This box is a traveler's delight. It has a face mask, hand lotion, body lotion, shower gel, shampoo, conditioner, haircare serum, hair mask, and so many more things. It probably costs hundreds of dollars!"

"It's alright," I replied. "I was going to sell these illegally if I ran out of money. Besides, I don't use most of them."

"Thank you," Champa said. "I'll only accept this if you let us pay for all your meals. That only seems fair."

Rory and Desmond nodded in agreement.

"Guys, it's really not a big deal," I told them. "You don't need to pay for my meals."

"We insist," Rory replied.

"Please, Keira," Desmond added. "I really like your gift. But I will only accept it if you comply with our terms and conditions."

I smiled. "Okay. But I'll still contribute to the groceries and other purchases. Okay?"

"Deal," all three of them said in unison.

I was secretly happy that Rory, Champa, and Desmond wanted to repay me. Back home, my classmates and friends expected me to give them AMZ products for free. At first, I didn't mind it, but when some of them started demanding freebies, I didn't know how to refuse.

"Desmond, how did you get interested in creating self-care products?" I asked.

"I have very sensitive skin," Desmond answered. "But I love indulging in self-care. Instead of complaining about other products, I decided to create my own. I haven't commercialized any of these yet, but I might do that in the future if my dream of becoming a professional gamer doesn't work out."

"Wow!" Rory exclaimed. "You mean video games, right? What games do you play? Do you develop them too?"

"I only play," Desmond replied. "My dad's company develops them. I play everything, but I like the shooter saga games the best."

I turned to Champa. "Do you play too?"

Champa nodded. "I'm nowhere as good as Des though. Besides, I can play for a maximum of an hour or two. Beyond that, I get bored. I start watching reels when that happens. And when I feel guilty for being glued to the screen too much, I do carpentry."

"You both have such unique hobbies," Rory stated. "My interests are very common and boring: swimming, camping, and sketching."

"I don't understand how a hobby, or anything, can be generalized as boring or weird," Champa said. "I like insects and carpentry, but everyone else calls me weird. They say 'Live a little. Go to parties.' Well, guess what? I think parties are boring. But that's just my opinion."

"Champa makes a very valid point," I pitched in. "My friends call me boring, too, for not being interested in makeup or beauty. I don't understand why."

Rory nodded. "I don't drink. Everyone except my closest friends call me boring because of that."

"We are not boring," Desmond said, pointing to the three of us. "That's why we don't hang out with them but with each other. On that note, let's raise a toast."

I giggled. "Wait, let me get us some water."

When I came back with four glasses of water, Desmond spoke. "To us, the four most interesting teenagers ever. And we'll not let anyone else make us feel otherwise."

We laughed and shouted, "Cheers."

We drank our water and continued our conversation.

"So, Desmond and Champa, why did you sign up for the Mobile Rehab?" Rory asked. "What kind of screen addicts are you?"

Champa and Desmond looked at each other. I saw a hint of panic on their faces for a moment. But it disappeared so fast, I may have imagined it.

"Gaming addict," Desmond said.

"Bathroom screen addict," Champa answered. "That means, I take my phone to the bathroom and stay there for a long time. And short videos on social media."

"I'm hooked to short vids too," I confessed. "I doom scroll more often than I want to. Maybe it's a good thing I ended up in Mobile Rehab."

"What do you mean by 'ended up'?" Desmond asked.

I smiled. "I came to Hong Kong for a different reason. Rory convinced me to sign up for the Mobile Rehab when we met at the airport for the first time."

Champa giggled. "Ah, so Rory's the reason you're in this mess."

"I didn't know we'd get duped," Rory said. "Anyway, back to why I signed up for the program. For me, it's *all* of the above. I can't sleep at night without my phone. Last night was an exception, because I was so tired from the journey."

"I doubt *any* teenager can sleep without their phone," I said. "Even before exams, when we pull all-nighters at the library, all of us take breaks to bury our faces in our phones instead of napping. We're all too addicted."

Rory nudged me. "You sound like Mr. Yu."

I shoved him playfully. "I don't nag like that annoying man. I accept that some of his points are valid, though. But, gosh, he didn't have to diss us so badly."

Everyone laughed. We continued talking about different things, as they let their face masks work their magic on their skin. We learned that Desmond and Champa were seventeen—two years younger than Rory and me—and went to a private residential high school in Canada. Desmond lived with his dad in Singapore and Champa was from India. They only went home for the holidays.

Next, we talked about the most interesting thing about ourselves. We tried playing truth or dare, but everyone was too lazy to do dares, so we stuck to chatting.

"No way," Rory exclaimed. "Desmond was in a movie? Which one?"

"It was a small role," Desmond said, going red in the face. He glared at Champa for revealing this information. "*The Videogamers*. Have you heard of it?"

I nodded. "It was a rage among my friends. I watched it, too, but I still can't remember who you played. Sorry."

"Des, you were so forgettable in the movie, people don't even recognize you," Champa teased.

"No, no," I clarified. "I went there with my boyfriend—I mean, ex-boyfriend. It was at a time when we were more interested in each other than the movie."

I felt the blood rush to my face as I recalled my date with Diego. It was back when we were totally into each other and oblivious to everything else. We held hands during the entire movie, and I couldn't remember anything that was happening on the screen.

"You didn't miss much," Desmond said. "It was a stupid film I was forced to be a part of because the original actor backed out at the last moment. I did it for my dad, who produced the movie. I didn't really enjoy being a part of it, though. The lead actors were arrogant and treated me badly."

"You don't have to talk about it if you don't want to," Rory said. "But when I saw you yesterday, I kind of knew you were a celebrity. You have that star quality."

Desmond blushed. "You're flattering me. Now, can we talk about anyone else except me?" He turned to Champa. "Did you tell them you're an Olympiad winner?"

Champa made a face. "Not the winner, but the second runner-up. And it was the junior biology Olympiad three years ago. I didn't even pass the qualifier after that."

"That's still very impressive," I said. "Isn't it a national-level competition?"

"Yes," Desmond answered for Champa. "Second runner-up in the entire country. Winning the bronze medal is amazing. Value your achievements."

"He's right," I said. "I stood third in a citywide singing contest last year. That's how I was able to afford this trip. My mother wasn't impressed, but I was happy."

"All of you are amazing, but I literally take the cake for the best story," Rory declared. "I won the cheesecake-eating contest at the Recharge Café a few months ago. I finished seventeen slices of the treat in under ninety minutes."

We all gasped. "You're kidding, right?"

Rory shook his head. "My former coach was a horrible person who almost got me suspended from college. That's a long story for another day. Anyway, he forbade me from eating desserts. When I quit swimming, the first thing I did was go to my favorite café and order *all* the flavors of their cheesecakes. I didn't even know there was a contest going on until I won it."

"Whoa, that's unbelievable," I said, trying to imagine the scene.

Rory chuckled. "I'm never doing that again. I was sick for a week after eating so much."

"Were you able to eat cheesecake after that?" I asked. "I don't think I could."

Rory nodded, smiling. "Surprisingly, yes. I had two slices the day before I got on my flight to Hong Kong."

All four of us laughed.

"This calls for a group photograph," Desmond said.

"Let's take one with my Polaroid," I suggested.

We huddled together for the selfie and smiled brightly.

Champa squealed. "We look so good. I have an idea. I'll be right back."

She got two small wooden dice and stuck them to the photo with some glue to make a stand. "There, that's perfect. I'll place it on the windowsill."

"That looks great," we all agreed.

We chatted until we decided to call it a night. We were to wake up early tomorrow to take the ferry to Lantau Island. I fell asleep the minute I hit my futon.

***

Later, a sudden noise woke me up. I was shocked to see the shadow of a man tiptoeing toward me with something in his hand. Was it the man who'd been following us earlier? How did he get inside our apartment?

I opened my mouth to scream, but he gently put his hand over my mouth.

"Keira, it's just me, Rory," he whispered. "I'm sorry I woke you up."

I heaved a sigh, relieved. "Thank goodness. You almost gave me a heart attack."

"Sorry," Rory said again. "Go back to sleep."

"I can't," I told him, still whispering. "I'm wide awake now."

Champa hadn't stirred even a little during this whole commotion.

"Why are you still awake?" I asked. "And why are you carrying that phone? It doesn't work."

"I couldn't sleep, so I was trying to switch this thing on again."

"Any luck?" I asked.

Rory sighed. "None whatsoever."

"Do you want to make some coffee? I don't want to wake up Champa."

Rory chuckled. "This place is very small. We can hear each other from any corner of the house."

"True."

"But I'm still game for a cup of coffee," Rory said. "Even if the caffeine will keep me wide awake for the rest of the night."

"We can make instant noodles then. Let's keep the lights off though. I'll switch on my flashlight."

We poured hot water into our instant noodle cups and waited for the noodles to cook.

I recalled the times when my father and I would stay up late and talk. We'd do that when I fought with my mother or Sebastian. A warm bowl of instant ramen with some hot sauce and catupiry cheese, along with my father's "dad jokes," were enough to forget all my problems.

After eating, I'd pour my heart out to him. He'd make me feel better by just listening to me while stroking my hair. Soothed, I'd fall asleep, and he'd tuck me back in bed. The next morning, I'd wake up feeling fine, completely forgetting about what had made me so angry. I'd make up with my mother or Sebastian instantly, and all would be well again.

But now, I had no one on my side.

"I miss my phone," Rory admitted, breaking the silence.

I miss my Pai, I wanted to say but stayed quiet.

"I wasn't always like this, you know? I had a life beyond my cell phone." He paused and sighed. "Now, I feel lost without it. Isn't that stupid?"

I shook my head. "No, it's not stupid. I started browsing through my phone mindlessly at night whenever I was upset with my friends, now ex-boyfriend, or family. Then, it became a habit."

"And I started when..." Rory paused before speaking again. "Hey, I remember something I need to complete. Do you mind if I eat my noodles in my room?"

I shook my head. "Go ahead."

"Sorry."

"It's alright, Rory. You don't have to apologize."

Rory went back to his room with his noodle cup, and I sat on the kitchen counter and ate mine. I tried to use the chopsticks that came with the packet, but the noodles kept slipping away. After a few minutes, I set the chopsticks aside and drank the noodles and broth. I could have eaten with a fork, but this was way more fun. And it was helping me keep my mind away from my problems.

"Um, can I join you again?" Rory asked, coming back into the kitchen.

"Sure."

He sat on the floor and drank the noodle soup like me. I hopped down from the counter and sat in the tiny empty space next to him, and we continued eating without talking. The only sounds in the room were of us slurping the noodles together.

"That wasn't tasty," I commented when we finished. "But it was a lot of fun."

"Yes. I felt like a kid again."

I laughed. "You have a noodle stuck to your chin."

"Thanks." Rory wiped his chin with the back of his hand. "And you have broth all around your mouth."

I got up and washed my mouth at the sink.

"So, did you complete your errand?" I asked Rory.

"Yeah. I mean, no." Rory paused for a moment and washed his hands. "I didn't have any work. I just felt uncomfortable about continuing our conversation earlier. But I didn't want to be rude, either, so I came back. Are you planning to sleep now?"

"Nope. I'm not sleepy. You?"

Rory smiled. "Me neither."

"Doom scrolling would have really helped us right now," I said.

"Tell me about it. It's like magic." Rory fished Yuan's phone from his pocket. "Should we pretend this dead device is like a real smartphone?"

I giggled. "That'd be lame, but let's do it." I pretended to switch on the phone. "So, what would we watch first?"

"Lip-sync videos."

I laughed. "Done."

Rory and I took turn lip-syncing the lyrics to popular songs on social media. We looked ridiculous with our over-the-top expressions and head-banging, but we didn't care.

All of a sudden, Rory started reciting an action rhyme, imitating a hideous viral dance, and I couldn't stop laughing.

"What's that?" I asked, still in a fit of giggles.

"The algorithm decided to show me this now," Rory answered, continuing to move his hands and legs about in a robotic manner. Supposedly, he was a robotic housefly.

In response, I sang a popular ad jingle for a hot sauce brand in the same chipmunk voice as the advertisement.

Rory plopped on the floor, unable to control his laughter. "Keira, what in the world is that?"

I just continued my hilarious antics in response.

For the next half hour, we tried to outdo each other by re-enacting popular online videos to see who was funnier.

"Alright, I can't take it anymore," I said, clutching my sides. "If I laugh again, I will burst."

"Same here. Let's call it a night."

"Okay," I said. "Good night."

"Hey, Keira," Rory called out to me softly.

"Yeah?"

"Thanks for tonight," Rory said. "I didn't want to be alone without my cell phone."

"I had fun too," I replied. I added with a laugh, "We have watched some *crazy* stuff on the internet, haven't we?"

Rory laughed with me. "Maybe that realization will help me overcome my phone addiction."

"You know what I feel? I don't think we'd be so attached to our phones if we had the right people to talk to. It's our loneliness that makes us so dependent on our phones."

Rory nodded. "Yes, you're right. I doom scroll to try to fill a void in my life, but I never succeed." He continued quietly. "I forgot that empty feeling last night and tonight when I was with you. So, thank you."

I was moved by Rory's sincerity and didn't know how to respond. No one had expressed their appreciation toward me in words except my father. I craved to hear comforting words from my mother and brother, but they thought showing their emotions made them weak.

I came back to the present when I realized Rory was still waiting for me to say something.

"Rory, remember how you told me I have the knack to say the right thing and you find it hard to respond? Well, the tables have turned this time."

CHAPTER 11

Rory

I tiptoed back into the bedroom as softly as I could, surprised Desmond was still fast asleep. I could hear Champa snoring from the living room. Keira and I had tried to be as quiet as possible with the lights off. But our laughter was loud, and we thought we had woken up the other two. However, they were blissfully asleep.

I closed my eyes, hoping to fall asleep, but Keira's words kept ringing in my ears.

It's our loneliness that makes us depend on our phones.

My mind drifted back to the honest conversation I'd had with my best friend, Tina, when she'd dropped me at the airport for this trip. Though she assured me everything was alright between us, it was hard to believe her.

I had been a terrible friend to her in the past, and she'd stopped talking to me. But we had made up recently—or so I thought. Tina was still friendly with me when we met up, but our friendship wasn't the same as before.

I knew it was my fault that she didn't confide in me anymore or spend as much time with me, but I wished she'd give me a chance to explain my side of the story.

Maybe, I'd stop feeling guilty toward her.

Maybe, I'd stop feeling so lonely.

Maybe I wouldn't have to depend on a stupid mobile device for comfort.

This was all because of *her*.

I clenched my fists and shut my eyes tightly to get rid of these useless thoughts. I fished the dead phone from my pocket and pretended it worked. I replayed my favorite online videos in my mind until I fell asleep.

***

"Ror, are you still going to Tina's grandparents' orchard this summer?"

"Yes, Har. We've talked about this several times. You can come too. Tina's grandparents will be happy."

Harriet shook her head. "No, it's fine. You have fun."

"Why not?" I asked. "We can have fun *together*. It's the last summer before we head off to college."

"Tina might not like it."

"Come on, Harriet. Tina invited you herself. Why wouldn't she want you, one of her best friends, to come?"

"It's fine. You both can enjoy it without me."

"Okay, the invite is still open though. Let me know if you change your mind."

"When are you leaving?"

"Tonight."

"Cool. I'll miss you, boyfriend," Harriet said, hugging me.

I held her tightly. "Me, too, girlfriend. Though we don't have to. If you change your mind and come with us."

"How can I? You made plans without talking to me. You informed me at the last moment."

"What? You were there when all three of us decided. You told Tina you were excited to visit the orchard."

Harriet pushed me angrily. "What else was I supposed to do? You never care about what *I* want."

"Of course I do."

She pinched my cheeks. "I know you do. I'm just joking, okay?"

I sighed. "I never get your jokes."

"Nor do you get me," she mumbled under her breath, loud enough for me to hear. But I pretended I didn't.

Instead, I embraced her again. "I'll call you on my way tonight."

I dialed Harriet's number several times while driving to Tina's grandparents' place, but she didn't pick up the calls.

After half an hour, she called me back. "Ror, have you left yet? Can you go tomorrow? I'll come with you."

"I'm on my way already. Why don't you drive down tomorrow?"

"Can't you come back?" Harriet whined. "How far are you?"

"It's an easy route to drive," I said, trying to convince her.

"I had an accident, Rory."

"What? When? Are you okay?"

"Yes," Harriet replied. "But I'd really like it if you were with me tonight."

Without another word, I made a U-turn and drove back to Harriet's house. Her mother opened the door.

"Mrs. Shelby, Harriet told me she had an accident," I said. "Is she alright? Is she inside?"

Harriet's mother frowned. "She didn't mention any accident to me."

"I told you how a bike hit my car earlier, Mom," Harriet said, coming downstairs from her room. "He almost broke one of my rearview mirrors."

"That hardly qualifies as an accident," Mrs. Shelby scolded. "Poor Rory. He looks so worried."

Harriet smiled. "I may have exaggerated a teeny bit. It's okay. Rory loves me. Don't you, Rory?"

I nodded mutely.

Mrs. Shelby laughed. "Alright, I'll leave you lovebirds alone. Harriet, keep your room door open."

"You should have told me you were okay," I said when we were in Harriet's room. "I wouldn't have come running like this."

"How else would I know if you truly loved me?"

"Har, I've told you many times that it's Tina's grandfather's birthday tomorrow. Gramps is very close to me. He treats me like his own grandson. I really wanted to go early and help them before the party."

"Sorry," Harriet said, sulking. "I didn't ask you to drive back. That's on you."

I sighed. I knew there was no point arguing with Harriet. She would never see things from my perspective.

"Be ready by six in the morning tomorrow," I said. "We need to leave early to avoid traffic."

Harriet nodded. "I'll be ready. I promise."

The next morning, Harriet surprised me by showing up at my doorstep at half past five. I was dressed and ready to leave. She said we should take her car, and I agreed. I thought she felt bad about last night but didn't broach the subject.

Harriet drove quietly. She was never a morning person and couldn't function without a cup of coffee. She had a large one to go but hadn't had the chance to drink it. I offered to drive but she refused.

To my utter shock, Harriet turned on the road leading to the airport. Before I could stop her, she had pulled over at the parking lot.

"What the hell, Harriet? Why are we at the airport?"

"Surprise!" Harriet said, waving two plane tickets in front of my face. "We're going on a trip. A romantic getaway to Calgary. Just the two of us."

I shook my head vehemently. "No. I'm going to Gramps's birthday party."

"I spent a fortune on these," Harriet cried. "Can't you miss a measly party for me?"

"You lied and tricked me into coming with you," I snarled.

"I didn't lie," Harriet insisted. "It was a part of my surprise plan. Please, Ror. I spent all my part-time job earnings on this. I really wanted to do something nice for us."

"You should have discussed it with me. If you wanted to surprise me, you could have picked any other date, *after* tomorrow. I've mentioned Gramps's birthday at least a dozen times in the past week."

"I'm really sorry you'll miss Gramps's party," Harriet said, tears rolling down her cheeks. "It's just that I really need you right now."

I hated seeing my girlfriend cry. I removed my seat belt and leaned forward, putting my arms around her. "Alright, don't cry. We'll try to work this out."

"My grandmother is dying, Ror. The doctors have asked us to be prepared for the worst."

I patted Harriet's back softly. "I'm sorry to hear that."

"So, I need this getaway badly. Please? It's just for two days."

"Wouldn't you rather stay back and spend time with your grandmother?" I asked.

"She's in the critical unit, Rory. And this stress is killing me. I need a breather."

I sighed, knowing it was useless to argue with my stubborn girlfriend. "Fine. I'll come with you."

Harriet wiped her tears. "Yay! Thank you."

"What do I tell Gramps?"

"Lie to him. Tell him my grandmother lives in Calgary, and she's really sick and wants to see me. Also, mention that I don't have anyone else to take me, as both my parents are traveling on urgent work."

I laughed. "Wow. You've thought of everything."

Harriet just shrugged in response.

I called Gramps and let him know I couldn't make it. After hanging up, I followed Harriet into the airport. She was in a great mood, chatting and joking the whole time. I tried to match her cheerfulness but couldn't, because I felt really guilty for canceling on Gramps at the last minute.

However, when we reached Calgary, Harriet started behaving coldly. She stopped talking to me and responded in monosyllables. She did this often, and I usually dismissed her behavior as mere mood swings. But today, I was furious. I had canceled my plans for her, and she was treating me terribly.

"What happened?" I asked. "Why are you in a bad mood?"

"I'm fine."

"You don't seem fine," I said. "You didn't even respond when I asked you if you needed to use the bathroom at the airport."

"You're creating a scene. Let's talk when we get to the hotel."

We checked into the hotel, though I didn't want to. It didn't feel right staying in the same room with my girlfriend overnight. She should not have booked this without my consent.

I followed Harriet to the elevator and to the room. But when she opened the door, I stayed put at the entrance. "Harriet, I can't go inside with you."

"Why not?"

"We need to talk first. Let's go someplace quiet. Please."

We went to the emergency stairway.

"What's your problem?" Harriet asked.

"You," I replied angrily. "*You're* my problem. You haven't spoken two words to me since we landed, and you expect me to stay with you in the same room overnight?"

Harriet scoffed. "You're overreacting as usual. When did I not respond?"

"Let's see. I asked you if you were hungry, wanted to use the bathroom, needed more coffee, if we were taking a cab... Need I go on?"

Harriet shrugged nonchalantly. "And I answered, 'yes' or 'no.' Because they are yes or no questions."

I sighed. "We're supposed to be here on a so-called romantic getaway that you planned. I've lied to Gramps and everyone else I care about for you. Can't you honor that for once?"

"You don't need to do me a favor by being here with me. You can go back home. I never forced you into this."

"Please stop it!" I screamed, banging my fist hard into the wall in the stairway. My knuckles started bleeding and hurt really badly, but I felt numb inside. "I can't do this anymore."

Harriet started sobbing. "Why are you getting violent? I did so much for us, and—"

I left without listening to another word.

***

I woke up and sat on my bed, gasping for air.

Great. I didn't let these horrible memories of *her* cloud my mind when I was awake, so they decided to haunt me during my sleep.

All I wanted was some peace.

And that seemed impossible because of *her*.

CHAPTER 12

Keira

I woke up with a start. What a weird dream that was. My ears ached again because I'd forgotten to apply the drops tonight. I put the ear drops in and tried to fall asleep again, but I couldn't stop thinking about my strange dream.

I was back home from Hong Kong, and Diego was waiting for me at the airport with a bouquet of flowers. Standing next to him were Sebastian, Savio, Marina, and my mother. Mom held out her arms, and I ran into them, engulfing her in a big warm hug.

She held me tightly. "I missed you. How could you just take off like that without talking to me first? Where did you go?"

"I went to Hong Kong. I visited all the places Dad used to talk about."

She kissed my forehead tenderly. "I'm glad you had fun. Come, let's go home."

"What's Diego doing here?" I whispered. "I won't forgive him. He's cheating on me."

"I gave him a piece of my mind when I heard what he did," Mom replied. "He told me it was a misunderstanding and begged me to give him a chance to explain to you. That's why I agreed to bring him along." She squeezed my shoulder reassuringly. "If he is cheating on you, please remember it's not your fault. It's his. You're my beautiful daughter who deserves the best."

My eyes welled up. "Thanks, Mom. I was so scared you'd blame me again."

She ruffled my hair lovingly. "I'm sorry I did that. Now, go and listen to what Diego has to say."

I was surprised about my mother's behavior. It had been months since she'd embraced me. The last time we hugged was during my birthday party last year. Besides, she had never called me beautiful. She must have really missed me these past two weeks.

I hugged my brother and my friends one by one. They seemed genuinely happy to see me.

"I'm always on your side, bestie," Marina whispered.

What happened to the girl who'd blamed *me* for my boyfriend kissing someone else two weeks ago? The exact words she'd used were, "you don't try hard enough to keep your man, Keira."

"I'm sorry for being selfish," Savio said. "I shouldn't have brought up my feelings for you."

I wanted to respond, *No, you shouldn't have. More than that, you had no right to say, "I like you despite your average looks." That was horrible of you.* But I kept quiet. I didn't want to start a fight right now.

"Aren't you glad I told on you to our mother?" Sebastian asked. "See, everything worked out."

I still didn't approve of my brother telling on me. I had pleaded with him not to say anything to our mother yet. But he hadn't listened. If I were in his place, I'd have kept my twin's secret. I'd have had his back, because that's what siblings do.

It was like none of it had happened.

Like I hadn't seen Diego kiss someone else.

Like my brother and friends hadn't taken his side.

And like my mother had never blamed me or essentially called me ugly.

"Keira." I heard Diego call my name. He placed the bouquet of red roses in my hands. "Shall we go?"

I was quiet as I followed Diego to his car and during the drive. He pulled over at the botanical garden parking lot. This was where we'd become a couple three years ago. Right after, we had our first date. We got burgers next door and took a stroll in the botanical garden. And that was when we kissed for the first time, watching the sunset. It had been perfect.

Diego opened the door and held it for me. He extended his hand, but I didn't take it. I got out of the car, and he closed the door and locked it. I didn't like his overly chivalrous behavior but didn't say anything.

"Are you hungry?" Diego asked.

I shook my head. "No. I don't want to eat now. Let's talk first. Didn't you bring me here for that?"

Diego took a deep breath. "Keira, I'm not cheating on you."

I scoffed. "Oh please. I saw you both—"

"Please let me finish," Diego interrupted. "What you saw was me checking if something went into her eyes. It turned out to be glass dust, and her eye is injured." He showed me her photo on his phone. "See, she is wearing an eyepatch."

"Oh."

Diego placed both his hands on my shoulders. "I would never ever cheat on you. You're too precious to me. I can't imagine my future without you."

I cupped his face with my hands, pulled him closer and kissed him. There were fireworks in my belly just like that first time. I knew he felt the same way, because I could hear his heart beating rapidly at the same pace as mine.

When we pulled away, I smiled as I lost myself in his warm coffee brown eyes. *Rory Matthews.*

A shudder went down my spine. What was *Rory* doing in my dream? And why was my heart racing right now thinking about it?

It made no sense.

Sure, Rory was really good-looking, and I knew I wasn't the only one who thought so. Moreover, he was charming and had a magnetic personality. He was also fun to hang out with and caring. But I barely knew him.

Was I so desperate for a distraction from the reality of being cheated on?

I tried to get Rory out of my mind and imagine my mother's arms around me again and that loving look in her eyes. I craved her affection more than anything else in this world. But even when I did everything she wanted me to, including stuffing my bra, which I hated so much, she didn't pay much attention to me. She had eyes only for my brother.

I closed my eyes, hoping to relive the dream hug I'd gotten from her in the airport. But I only heard her hurtful words, which pierced my heart time and again. I wiped my eyes with the back of my hand. There was no point building fake castles in the air. The reality was my mother didn't appreciate me for who I was.

The one person who had accepted me was my father, but he was no longer in this world. All I could do was see this city he'd loved so much through his eyes and recall his excitement when he spoke about his memories with me. Thinking about him made my tears flow even harder like they always did.

I still missed him like crazy.

***

I woke up to Rory, Desmond, and Champa arguing.

"Please, Rory, I haven't been able to go since we came here," Desmond said. "I can't poop without looking at the phone."

"Guys, haven't you heard of ladies first?" Champa asked. "Watching reels while doing my business has become a habit for me. I can't get rid of it."

"I promise I'll be quick," Rory said, rushing to the bathroom and ignoring Champa. "I'll be out before you know it. Sorry, Desmond. I haven't been able to go the past two days, either."

Desmond shook his head. "I can't believe we're fighting over a dead phone."

"I agree it's pathetic," Champa said. "But I'm desperate right now."

I thanked my stars that I hadn't gotten into the habit of taking my phone with me to the bathroom. My brother had that habit, and it was annoying.

"And madam, you can't use the *ladies* card whenever you feel like," Desmond said to Champa. "Not when you preach about gender equality at other times."

Champa threw her pillow at Desmond, which turned into a pillow fight. They chased each other around the small living room, laughing.

But the second Rory came out of the bathroom, Champa went in and tried to close the door. Desmond pushed it from outside, screaming it was his turn. Champa reached out to tickle Desmond, who let go of the door immediately. She locked the door, laughing triumphantly.

Desmond sulked and glared at Rory, who shrugged. "I kept my promise."

Within a few seconds, Champa was back in the living room.

"Des, I'll let you go first," she said. She stuck her tongue out at him. "But don't forget I won."

"Those two are hilarious," Rory said, taking a sip from his water bottle. I watched his Adam's apple bob up and down as he swallowed the liquid.

I nodded, my face feeling hot at the sight of his handsome face. "They are."

"Did you sleep well?" he asked.

I nodded again, not meeting his eyes.

"Cool," he replied. "What's for breakfast?"

"Desmond and I are making omelets," Champa answered. "We're planning to add extra spice to the food today. I hope that's okay."

I gave her a thumbs-up. "That's perfect. Feel free to use my hot sauce. You can empty it if you like."

Rory laughed. "Let's not get too crazy. We don't want to burn our insides."

Champa giggled. "Don't worry, we won't go overboard."

After breakfast, we got dressed and walked to the ferry station. We were on time for the half past seven ride, which wasn't crowded. We even got seats on the deck. I enjoyed the feeling of the cool sea breeze on my face as I watched the deep blue ocean. The gentle waves calmed my mind as they danced on the surface rhythmically.

Next to me, Rory fell asleep quickly. His head swayed in different directions as he slept. He even hit his head on the seat edge but didn't wake up. When I felt him plop on my shoulder a few minutes later, I didn't move away. I let him rest comfortably.

As my heart raced and I felt my stomach flutter, I realized there was no point fighting it.

I had a crush on Rory Matthews.

CHAPTER 13

Rory

"Rory, wake up, we've reached the island." I heard Keira's voice. "We need to get off this ferry and catch the next one."

I sat up immediately, realizing that I was sleeping on Keira's shoulder.

"Sorry," I said. "That must have been uncomfortable."

"It wasn't as bad as your fly-robot dance," she joked.

I laughed. "The jingle in your chipmunk voice was *way* worse."

Keira laughed and shook her head. "Were you able to sleep at least a little bit last night?"

"Nope, your reel impressions haunted me all night," I deadpanned.

"Well, your head was heavy," Keira countered. "So, we're even."

I was glad Keira was back to her normal self. I'd been worried I'd said or done something that upset her because of how she hardly talked to me this morning. But I must have just misunderstood everything because of being so tired.

After waking up because of my nightmare earlier, I had allowed the suppressed memories to come back. They had gushed into my mind, flooding it.

After my horrible fight with Harriet, I'd dragged myself to the nearest walk-in clinic to get my hand checked. Thankfully, nothing was broken. Then, I went to the airport hoping the airline would let me take the next flight home. However, the rescheduling fees were too high.

Dejected, I sat in the waiting area where I could be alone. I'd had a terrible headache, and I was famished. I got a burger and some coffee, but I was in too much pain to eat. My hand felt better, thanks to the medication, but my chest hurt a lot. I buried my face in my hands and wept silently, hoping the pain would flow away with my tears.

I stopped crying when I couldn't anymore. But the hollow feeling in my heart remained. I needed something to distract me. I fished out my phone from my pocket and started playing games. I got lost in the wonderful virtual world. When my hands were tired from tapping on the phone, I watched social media videos until it was time for my flight.

I dreaded seeing Harriet again, but I was determined not to fall for her tricks this time. When I checked in, I chose a seat on the last row, the ones she hated. She had tried calling me nine times that evening, and I had not picked up any of them. My phone beeped. It was a text message from her.

> **Harriet:** My grandmother is no more. I hope you're happy.

I felt really guilty and called her immediately. She cried uncontrollably as I tried to comfort her.

And we got back together.

Harriet used my guilt to her advantage for the rest of the time we were together. I felt dead on the inside when she came close to me or touched me. But I didn't break up with her. She wouldn't let me.

She continued being her usual moody self, but it didn't affect me anymore. To evoke a reaction from me, she became more violent. Every time she threatened me or treated me terribly, I hated myself more than the previous time. But I endured it because I blamed myself for making her become a monster. She ensured I did.

I lost interest in everything and everyone: my family, my friends, swimming, and camping. Only one thing gave me solace—my phone.

Even now, so many months after breaking up, I despised myself for allowing myself to go through that nonsense. There were many signs that my relationship with Harriet was toxic, even back when we had just started dating. But I had ignored all of them. I got sucked into her crap like a black hole. Until it was too late.

Way too late.

Because her toxicity was contagious, and it affected my friends.

If only I had put an end to it earlier, would I have been able to protect my loved ones from her wrath?

"Hey, look, a pink dolphin," Keira said, snapping me out of my reverie.

"Where?" I asked.

She turned in the direction where she'd see the animal. "Over there."

"Why don't you just point?" I asked, amused.

"We must not point at animals," Champa replied. "It can provoke them to attack."

"That's for creatures that can see us," Desmond argued. "The dolphins are far away."

I nodded. "Exactly."

"Anyway, there they are," Keira said. "There are three now."

I photographed the beautiful pink sea creatures as they pranced about in the sea. I also shot a few videos.

"You'll have to send me those later," Keira whispered to me.

I nodded. "Okay, but why are you whispering? The dolphins can't hear you."

She laughed. "I'm just used to following wildlife-watching rules, okay?"

"I know. I was just teasing you."

"I really miss my phone," Desmond wailed. "This camera is not half as good as on my smartphone."

"While we are on the subject of smartphones, should we expose the Hong couple's scam on social media when we get back?" Champa asked. "Or should we let it go, since we have a place to stay?"

"I'm of two minds," I answered. "I'm upset they conned us, but also relieved we're not on the streets."

"Let's think about it a bit more," Rory suggested.

Desmond nodded. "I agree. And here comes our next ferry."

***

I fell asleep again during the second ferry ride. But, this time, I leaned on the wall next to my seat. It had started drizzling and we sat indoors. Desmond woke me up when it was time to get off.

"Did you get any sleep at all last night?" he asked.

I shook my head. "No. That's why my head is killing me."

"Let's get some coffee," Desmond said.

"We might miss the bus," I replied.

"It's fine. There's one every ten minutes."

"Shouldn't we inform the girls first?" I asked, looking for Keira and Champa. I didn't see them anywhere.

"That little pop-up store might have coffee," Desmond said.

He probably didn't hear my question because of the noise. The tourists and the store owners were really loud. Though the ferries weren't crowded, there were many people waiting for the bus to Tian Tan Buddha, more commonly known as Big Buddha.

"Where are the girls?" Desmond asked when we stood in line.

I chuckled. "I asked you that earlier." I pointed to the green bus that had just left. "Hey, isn't that the bus we need to take? Do you think Keira and Champa are there?"

Desmond laughed. "Maybe."

"They'll wait for us at the entrance."

"Or if they're still here, we'll wait for them," Desmond said.

As we continued to wait, I looked around. Another ferry arrived and more people came to the already crowded place. Most of them headed toward the buses, but some of them stopped at the pop-up stores.

There were about five or six stores in the area. One of them was a convenience store that sold things tourists might have forgotten to pack. All the others were food/beverage stalls. There was a coffee shop, a small bakery, and three stores that sold fresh snacks I didn't recognize. Most of the store signboards/menus were in Chinese.

"Excuse me," two girls called out to Desmond and me. They looked like they were the same age as us. "Are you a couple?"

"Sorry, what do you mean?" Desmond asked.

One of the girls giggled. "If not, would you like to spend the day with us? It'll be fun."

"You both are our type," the other one added.

I bit back a smile. It had been a while since I'd been hit on. It used to happen a lot when I represented the university for swimming contests. But after I'd quit, not many people paid attention to me.

"Thanks, but I'll politely decline," I said.

"Thank you for asking us, though," Desmond added, bowing slightly.

"Can we get a photo with you, at least?"

Desmond and I posed for a photo with the girls. They thanked us and left. We saw them approach two other teenage boys. After a few minutes, the four headed to the bus together.

"Wow, what courage those girls have," Desmond stated.

I nodded. "True. And they made two new friends."

"You know, I was pretty popular in my school until I became an outcast."

I frowned. "Why would anyone make *you* an outcast?"

Desmond sighed. "I didn't do some things everyone else wanted me to. I paid a price for taking a stand."

"Yeah. Popularity is overrated. I'd choose real friends over it any day."

"Same here," Desmond agreed. "I don't know what I'd do without Champa."

It was our turn to order. We got our drinks and walked to a place with more shade. The sun was scorching right now. All traces of the rain earlier had disappeared. We finished our coffee and waited at the bus stop.

"The weather here is so unpredictable," I said, wearing my sunglasses. "It rains one minute, and the next it's blindingly sunny."

Desmond laughed. "Singapore is similar, so I'm pretty used to it. But, hey, this isn't as bad as Canada. There were times when I had to carry my winter jacket, raincoat, and summer shirts for a single trip."

I chuckled. "Touché. I know exactly what you're talking about. My city is like that too. Hey, why don't you and Champa come down to Strollfield sometime?"

"Thanks for inviting us. We'd love to. But my school is pretty strict about letting students outside the premises. They don't even allow us to date."

I looked at Desmond in disbelief. "Really? Which school is this?"

"Peaks N Valleys Residential School," Desmond replied. "It's a private school. Have you heard of it?"

I gasped. "You're from *the* PNVRS? Don't you guys have a stellar record of students getting into the Ivies? Like a crazy thirty percent of your school get into the world's best universities, right?"

"Yep, that's the one. The Peaks Factory."

I raised my eyebrow. "The Peaks Factory?"

"If you're not cut out for it, they discard you like a defective product in a factory," Desmond explained. "They accept only the peaks and disregard the valleys. It's the students that are good. Not the school itself."

I followed Desmond onto the bus, continuing our conversation. "You guys probably deal with a lot of pressure."

Desmond nodded as he took a seat in the front row. "Yep. And I hate it. But my parents and their parents went there. So, I have no choice."

I sat down next to him. "Wow, I had no idea you had it so bad. We public schoolers were envious of private school students. In our eyes, you have it easy."

Desmond smiled. "And we're jealous of you and your seemingly carefree lives."

I thumped him on the back in a friendly manner. "It'll get better, man. You'll be in college soon." I took my pocket notebook from my bag, tore a sheet of paper off, and wrote my phone number on it. "If you need to vent, just text, or call me."

Desmond borrowed my notebook and pen and scribbled his number. "And here's mine."

Desmond and I chatted nonstop during the bus journey.

And it was a real pity the ride was only for an hour.

CHAPTER 14

Keira

Champa and I sneaked out to the boat's deck in the rain during our second ferry ride. It was just drizzling, but most passengers were indoors. The sun was shining brightly despite the rain.

"Are your ears better now?" Champa asked.

I nodded. "Yes. But they were terrible last night."

Champa patted lightly on my back. "I'm glad you're feeling better. I've seen my sister suffer from ear pain, so I know how painful it is." Suddenly, she squealed gleefully. "Look, a rainbow."

We jumped up and down like excited little kids and clicked selfies together. The rainbow's colors intensified with each photo Champa captured with her digicam. When it was most prominent, I took a couple frame-worthy pictures of both of us with my Polaroid camera.

I handed Champa one of the photographs and wrote my phone number and email address on its back. "Here you go. Can you send me the rest of your photos?"

"Yes, of course." Champa hugged the photo close. "We look so adorable. I'm going to frame this."

I smiled. "I know, right? It's perfect."

We both admired the photograph for a few more minutes. Champa and I had our arms around each other and grinned widely. Our faces glowed along with the brilliant colors of the rainbow and the turquoise blue ocean in the background.

"Oops, we forgot to call the boys," I said, remembering Rory and Desmond suddenly.

Champa rushed to get them. But she came back within a few seconds. "Both are fast asleep."

I giggled. "We'll rub our photo in their faces and make them jealous."

Champa high-fived me. "I'd love that."

We watched the rainbow together in silence until it disappeared. It stopped raining when it was almost time to reach Lantau Island. Champa and I went to wake up Rory and Desmond, but people blocked our way. Hence, we were forced to get off the ferry without the guys.

The crowd was worse on the island. The place was in chaos, because there was no one to direct tourists. People had flocked near the buses, the pop-up stores, and the ferry.

Champa and I held hands, not wanting to lose each other. We wore our backpacks in the front for safety. The boys were nowhere in sight.

"Let's wait in the bus," I suggested. "The guys will join us."

Champa gave me a thumbs-up. It was almost impossible to converse over all the noise. When we searched for the bus, we saw a woman open another woman's backpack and steal her wallet. Instantly, Champa and I hugged our own bags closer to our bodies.

Another tourist also saw this and yelled at the top her voice, "Thief!"

The robber tried to escape but was caught. Many people crowded around them to witness the scene, blocking our view. We ran away from the commotion and got into one of the buses that was ready to leave.

"Does this bus go to Tian Tan Buddha?" Champa asked the bus driver, to ensure we were in the right vehicle.

The driver nodded and swiped our transport cards. I sat in the first row, while Champa reserved the second row for the guys. However, I had to give up my seat when an elderly couple got in. The driver closed the door and started the bus.

I sat down next to Champa. "We'll wait for the guys near the temple entrance."

"I didn't know the bus would leave so soon. I've been looking out the window and haven't seen Desmond or Rory."

I placed my hand on hers. "It's alright. I'm sure they're fine."

Champa placed her other hand on mine. "I'm actually excited it's just us. We can have a girls' day out."

I laughed. "That's a great plan."

"Do you want to sit near the window?" Champa asked.

I shook my head. "I'm good, thanks."

"Let me open it a bit more then." Champa slid the window effortlessly.

I noticed she had painted her nails turquoise blue.

"When did you have time to paint your nails?" I asked. "They look lovely."

Champa blushed. "Thanks. I did them this morning when I woke up early. They don't take much time. Do you want me to do yours?"

"No, thanks. I don't think it'd suit me."

Champa frowned. "Says who?"

I showed her my hand. "They're short and narrow."

"And lovely," she added.

"Oh come on."

"I'm serious," Champa replied. "You have slender fingers. Short nails match them perfectly. And bright colors will make them stand out even more. You should paint them! Only if you want to, of course."

"Okay, let's do that tonight. I'll try with my left hand first."

"Cool. We can remove it if you don't like it," Champa said.

I smiled. "Thanks for understanding."

"Of course. And thanks to you too."

I frowned, not understanding. "What do you mean?"

"You heard Desmond and me talking about looking for someone yesterday, right?"

I nodded.

"But you didn't say a word to Rory or either of us. Thank you for that."

"You don't have to thank me for that," I said. "It was nothing."

"Desmond and I had another motive to sign up for the Mobile Rehab," Champa stated. She added after a pause. "We needed an economic accommodation in Hong Kong away from our classmates."

I frowned. "Why away from your classmates?"

Champa sighed. "Desmond and I are outcasts. Our classmates didn't want us around during the school trip. We are facing the consequences of not succumbing to peer pressure."

"But you still came here, so your parents won't ask you questions," I reasoned.

She nodded. "Exactly. Our families think we are on our school trip. And we had to come here because it was really important to Desmond."

My heart went out to Champa. "Is it okay if I hug you?"

She nodded slowly, her eyes welling up.

I put my arms around her and pulled her close to me. She wept softly as I patted her back trying to comfort her.

"Sorry," Champa said, wiping her eyes. "I didn't mean to dampen the mood."

"Don't apologize," I replied. "All of us have our stuff." I took a deep breath. "I'm here because my boyfriend of three years cheated on me, and my family and friends blame me for it."

Champa raised her voice. "What?" She lowered it immediately. "Sorry, did I hear that right? Your family and friends blamed you for that a-hole cheating on you?"

I nodded.

"How much does it cost for a trip to Brazil?" Champa asked. "I'm coming there just to teach your so-called friends a lesson."

I laughed, delighted that she was on my side.

"I'm serious. I want to slap some sense into them."

I grinned widely. "Thanks. Just you saying that makes me feel better. I almost started wondering if I was as ugly—"

"Ugly? Seriously? They called *you* ugly?"

Well, no one *called* me ugly, but my mother made me feel that when she constantly compared my looks with Sebastian's. As a result, my friends belittled me too. But I didn't want to talk about my mother or friends right now.

Champa took the Polaroid photograph from her bag. "Look at this. You're freaking gorgeous. They're blind if they don't see that." She placed the picture back and took my hands in hers. "Repeat after me. I, Keira Delgado, am not ugly."

When I was about to do as she said, the bus came to a jerky halt. Luckily, we were fine because we had our seatbelts on.

"Sorry, the bus isn't working," the driver announced. "Everybody, please get off."

We got off the vehicle as instructed, hoping it would be repaired soon. However, other passengers told us the bus had completely broken down and would need to be towed to the garage. We were stranded here until another bus came to pick us up. But the biggest issue was there was no network in this area to call for help.

The driver informed us that he would check if he could get network elsewhere. He asked us to wait until he was back and to not go anywhere. We stood in the hot sun for more than thirty minutes as several buses passed by, but none of them stopped. We even spotted Rory and Desmond in one of them; however, they didn't see us waving at them and calling out their names.

"Ah, I can't believe it!" Champa shouted in frustration. "How could they not hear or see us?"

"They seemed to be in their own world," I replied.

"I'm thirsty and need to go to the bathroom," Champa wailed. "That's a horrible combination of feelings. Why did I have to finish all my water?"

I showed her my empty water bottle. "Same here. I know exactly what you mean."

"Ugh, this is so annoying. I'm so parched."

I gave Champa some hard candy I always carried with me. "Here, have this. This will keep us from getting dehydrated."

She hugged me sideways. "You're amazing. You think of everything."

I returned her embrace. "I'm glad you're here with me. Otherwise, I'd have gone crazy."

Champa opened her backpack and got some napkins and a bag of chips. She spread a napkin on the ground and signaled me to sit down. She sat next to me. Next, she took her umbrella and extended its handle to the maximum capacity. It was longer than the average umbrellas. She placed it in the space between us.

"Hopefully, this will keep us from melting," she said.

I opened my bag and took out the pocket fan I'd bought with the ear drops and switched it on the swing mode. "I don't know how long this will last, but if we don't use this, I might evaporate!"

Our fellow passengers stared at us, but we didn't care. We munched the chips and sucked on more candy. My bladder was reaching its limit, but I had no choice. I had to hold it in.

"Can you give me your copy of our rainbow selfie?" Champa asked.

I reached into my bag and handed her the photograph. She spent some time writing something on the back of the picture.

To keep my mind off my bladder, I thought about my new crush. I was happy because a new attraction meant I was over Diego. During my relationship, not once had I felt attracted to anyone else. But, before that, I'd had several crushes.

However, I was also excellent at keeping my crushes a secret. None of the boys I liked ever knew about it. And I didn't discuss my feelings with anyone else. Not even Marina or Sebastian. That's why I enjoyed it so much. It was all in my secret imaginary world. I didn't ever have to deal with reality.

"Here you go," Champa said, giving me back the photograph. "Read this every day, okay?"

I read it out aloud. "Words to repeat every day: I am drop dead gorgeous, and I will not pay heed to anyone who thinks otherwise. Reiterated by Champa Naidu."

"And here, I've signed below and added my contact details," Champa said. "Let's stay in touch and bitch about people who give us a hard time."

My eyes brimmed with tears. "Thank you. This means the world to me."

She wiped her own tears with the back of her hands. "The Hong couple may have conned us. But I really owe it to them for giving me a friend like you."

We held each other's hands and cried quietly.

This trip had made me realize I needed new friends.

And had given me them.

CHAPTER 15

Rory

Desmond and I paced back and forth, waiting for the girls near the entrance of the Big Buddha temple. Desmond looked at his pocket-sized clock numerous times, as if he was late for an appointment. It was past one in the afternoon, and there was no sign of Keira or Champa.

We heard two tourists talking about a bus that had gotten in an accident. My heart stopped for a moment. Desmond had turned pale too.

"Excuse me, sorry to bother you, but we heard you talk about a bus accident," I said to the tourists. "Do you have any more details? Was anyone hurt?"

The tourist shook her head. "No, we don't know any details. We also heard this from someone else."

We asked more people if they had any information, but we got varied responses. Some told us there was an accident with multiple casualties, some said that a bus had broken down, and others spoke of an irrelevant cable car incident.

"It's best we call the Lantau Island Tourist Information Desk," I said. "Maybe we could borrow someone's phone."

"Do you have the information desk's number?" Desmond asked.

I nodded proudly. "I wrote it down this morning."

"Cool, let's find someone who can help us."

We spent the next fifteen minutes stopping people and requesting they let us borrow their phones. But they ignored us and gave us suspicious looks.

Finally, a gentleman agreed to help us. However, he was also a foreign tourist like us without a local phone number and needed Wi-Fi to make a call.

"The nearest free Wi-Fi network spot is a five-minute walk from here," he said. "You can try to make a call from there. I must warn you though. I'm low on battery."

"Thanks, I'll go with you," I replied to the kind stranger. I turned to Desmond. "Please wait here for Keira and Champa."

The "five-minute walk" turned out to be longer, but I was in no position to complain. I quietly followed the gentleman, trying to ignore my hunger.

"Give me the number," he said, when we were outside a crowded restaurant. "I'll dial it for you, and you can talk."

A few moments later, he handed me his phone.

"Hi, I'm calling to get some information about a bus that was stranded on its way to Big Buddha."

"Good afternoon, sir. A bus broke down on its way to Tian Tan Buddha. Can you hold while I check if another vehicle went to pick up the passengers?"

Before I could agree, the call got disconnected because of the poor network connection. I tried several times to redial the number, but the line was busy. When I finally got through, the phone got switched off.

"Sorry, my device has run out of battery," the foreign tourist said. "Can you ask someone else for their phone? I don't want to be late for my guided tour."

"Sure, thanks for your help and sorry to keep you."

I ran back to the spot where Desmond was waiting. I was dejected that the girls weren't here yet.

"Did you get any information at all?" Desmond asked.

"The good news is that there was no accident," I answered. "The bus broke down. But the phone ran out of battery before I could find out if the girls got onto another bus or when they are expected to reach us."

"Well, it's a good thing no one is hurt. And that we could find out at least something."

I nodded. "I'm never traveling without my cell phone again. I know people survived without them before they were invented. But in to-day's world, they're a necessity."

"Ditto," Desmond agreed. "Without my phone, I feel like I've lost a body part!"

"Exactly."

My stomach growled again. Desmond noticed this and gave me a packet of chips.

"Thanks, I forgot to carry snacks today."

"No problem, I've got more if you want." Suddenly he pointed to the entrance. "The girls are here."

I ran toward Keira before I realized what I was doing. She was laughing and high-fiving Champa. Her lovely curls bounced around her pretty face. Her expression changed to one of startlement when she saw me.

"Rory, Desmond, why are you both running?" Champa asked.

"Rory ran, so I followed him," Desmond answered, panting. "I wondered why he took off like that. I thought he saw something scary."

"Do we look scary to you, Rory?" Keira teased. "Or did you miss us so much that you ran when you saw us?"

I felt the blood rush to my face, and my cheeks turned hot. "I—I just wanted to make sure it was you. I'm too hungry to see clearly."

Keira laughed. "Alright, let's say you were."

"We got discount coupons for twenty percent off for their lunch combo," Champa said. "The travel authorities felt sorry for our bus breaking down and gave us coupons."

"What are we waiting for?" Desmond asked. "Let's go."

I followed the three mutely, my heart racing. My cheeks still felt warm. I still didn't know why I ran like that. My legs started moving on their own when I saw Keira. At that moment, I didn't see anything or anyone else.

We stood in line to get lunch. Keira and Champa talked about their (mis)adventures of the day.

"Thank goodness the rescue bus driver stopped in between and let us use the bathroom," Keira said. "Otherwise, our bladders would have burst."

"And they got us each a water bottle and a banana," Champa added.

"They really went out of their way to ensure they don't get terrible reviews," Desmond said.

"Yes," Champa replied. "I'm impressed by their hospitality."

Within five minutes, it was our turn to be served lunch. Piping hot food was waiting for us at the table. There were four bowls of soup and crispy spring rolls to start off our meal.

The four of us ate in silence, enjoying the mild but flavorful dishes. The bean curd in the soup was melt-in-the-mouth soft. It was perfectly combined with a mushroom and soy-based broth. The spring rolls had an abundance of juicy vegetables.

Following the appetizer and the soup was a simple main course comprised of rice and two types of mixed veggie dishes. We felt light and happy after the wonderful meal.

"Should we get dessert?" I asked. "I overheard some tourists raving about the mango-filled rice dumplings."

Desmond got up from his seat immediately. "Of course."

We all laughed at his enthusiasm. After putting away our used plates and utensils, we bought the sweet treats. They were about to run out of them for the day, so we were lucky to grab the last few pieces.

"Oh my God," Keira exclaimed, taking a bite of the succulent dumplings. "We would have really regretted missing these delightful desserts. Thanks, Rory."

The rest of us were too busy eating to say anything. We were grateful to Desmond for getting two orders. One wouldn't have been enough.

After eating, we climbed up the 268 stairs to see the magnificent statue of Buddha seated on a lotus throne, made of bronze. His serene expression made me feel calm within.

I clicked pictures as I marveled at the intricate details of the statue. The Buddha's fingers, nails, and even palm lines, were carved perfectly. His hair, eyes, and other facial features looked real and life-like.

I sat down and sketched the statue in my notebook. I drew the outline first and added the details later. I shaded it to give it a three-dimensional effect. I didn't think I had done justice to the sculpted masterpiece, but I enjoyed working on it. After it was complete, I examined the drawing one last time before adding my initials at the bottom.

My hands itched to sketch more, so I looked around for inspiration. I saw Keira sitting quietly, with a subtle, beautiful smile on her face—the same one she'd had yesterday when we enjoyed Popsicles together.

On its own, my hand started drawing Keira. As I sketched her expressive eyes and beautiful face, my heart fluttered. It had been a while since I felt this way. And I liked it.

I had no plans for acting on my crush. Besides the fact that I'd probably never see her again after our trip, I wasn't ready for another relationship. My wounds from my previous one were still fresh and raw. And I had no idea when I would heal.

But I enjoyed the stomach flip flops I felt when I stole glances at her.

Or when our eyes met briefly.

Or when remembering the fun times we had together.

It brought an automatic smile to my face.

My crush was the perfect distraction I needed right now.

And it was my little secret.

Chapter 16

Keira

As I admired the massive Buddha statue, I remembered my father talking about it. He had said it was an inexplicable feeling that one had to experience themselves to understand. I got what he meant now. He had spent many hours here in this serene environment. The gentle breeze, the perfect temperature, and the calm surroundings were exactly as he had described it.

I, too, felt I could spend a long time here, doing nothing, enjoying my me-time. I was glad Rory was busy sketching, and Champa and Desmond had gone off on their own on some personal work. I wanted to experience this in solitude. Only one person was allowed in my space right now—my dearest Pai.

I let the thoughts from back home flow into my mind. Particularly the part I didn't want to think about ever again. My conversation with my mother just before I made the impulsive decision to take off to a foreign country without my phone.

I was still reeling from everything that had happened that day—me walking in on Diego kissing another girl; Sebastian, Marina, and Savio arriving at the same moment; me begging Sebastian not to tell our mother; Savio telling me he liked me despite my ordinary looks; and Marina blaming me for not "cleaning myself up" for my man.

My mother had called me, and I contemplated letting it go to voicemail.

But I answered it. "Hello?"

"Keira, are you coming home this weekend for summer break?"

"Yes, I plan to," I replied.

"Pretend like nothing happened during the party this weekend. Diego is performing solo, and I don't want any unnecessary drama. And don't cancel your summer holiday next week with your brother and his friends either."

I was furious. Here my heart was, broken, and my mother only cared about her party?

"You still want Diego to sing in your party after knowing what he did to me?"

"I told you it would happen someday, Keira. You never listen to me. How many times have I told you to fix yourself?"

I wanted to scream but spoke in the most even tone I could manage. "Are you telling me that it was my fault Diego cheated on me?"

"You could have avoided it," she said.

"Say it. Call me ugly. Go ahead!" I yelled.

"You can change that. We have the means to give you a new life. I've worked hard to ensure that. So, don't resist anymore. Say the word and I'll make appointments with everyone."

I disconnected the call, switched off my phone, threw it in the drawer, and locked it. Now, no one would be able to call me.

I'd looked at myself in the mirror.

"Fix what, huh?" I asked. "My big nose? My thin lips? Or my too-small breasts?" I let out an angry sob. "Pai, why did you leave me? Why did the only person who thought I was the most precious person in this world go away forever? It shouldn't have been you. If anyone had to go, it should have been her."

I felt terrible for uttering those words. I didn't mean it. I didn't want my mother to die. I might not see eye to eye with her, but I still admired her. I was proud of her. She had single-handedly grown into one of the most influential CEOs in our country. She was on her way to attaining international fame.

I decided I needed a break from everyone here. Without a second thought, I booked a ticket to Hong Kong, my father's most favorite place in the world. I texted my brother that I was not going home or on the holiday trip with him and asked him to inform everyone else. After that, I switched off my phone, stashed it in my drawer again, and left for the airport.

Back in the present, I was surprisingly okay after recalling the painful memory. Though I had decided to come here on a whim, it was right. I needed this space to calm down, collect my thoughts, and plan my future actions.

I got my notebook from my bag and wrote down the things I needed to do after getting back home.

>   1. Tell my mother I don't need fixing up. I'm happy with myself as is.
>
>   2. Be assertive with Sebastian. If he can't have my back as my twin brother, I'm not obligated to have his.
>
>   3. Quit the band.
>
>   4. Keep my distance from Savio and Marina. I don't need toxic

friends.

5. Break up with Diego. Duh.

6. Stay in touch with Champa, Rory, and Desmond.

7. Make new friends or find nontoxic people to hang out with
me.

All of a sudden, it started raining again. This time it was heavy. I put away my notebook and put on my rain jacket.

Rory came running toward me. "Do you want to run down the stairs?" he asked.

I laughed. "We might slip and fall if we race now."

"I meant together." He held out his hand.

I took it, my heart racing. We went down the stairs fast but carefully. I tried to keep my eyes on the steps, but they kept drifting toward Rory. He had rolled his jacket sleeves up, the veins on his strong athletic forearms prominent. I felt my cheeks getting hot despite the cold rain.

A loud rumbling of thunder caused other tourists to panic, and they ran down the stairs faster than before. Rory and I clutched our hands tighter and hurried to one side, letting people go before us. Once the path was clear again, we climbed down slowly.

A gust of wind blew away Rory's rain poncho hood. He let go of my hand to re-fasten the laces around his neck. I was disappointed we weren't holding hands anymore, but I casually placed mine in my jacket pocket. I couldn't make my attraction toward him obvious. Curious to see his reaction, I looked up at his face, but Rory was looking away. He didn't attempt to hold his hand out to me again either. And an awkward silence lingered between us.

When we reached the bottom of the stairs, it had almost stopped raining. But it was still cloudy. It was half past four and almost time for the monument to close. I stood on my tippy toes to see if I could spot Champa or Desmond. Neither Rory nor I had said a word. We'd talked easily before, so having to rack my brain to say something to him was a new feeling. But I had to break the silence fast, else my secret crush wouldn't remain so secret anymore.

I finally opened my mouth. "It stopped raining again. How many times has it been today?"

"Yeah," Rory responded. He added after a pause, "This was just the second time though."

I should have kept my mouth shut instead of sounding like an idiot. However, it would be rude not to reply. "True."

This was terrible. I had to stop behaving so weirdly. Rory might think I was giving him the cold shoulder. I didn't want him to get hurt because of me. I reminded myself we were friends.

"Do you want to check out the food markets in Tai O fishing village once Champa and Desmond come back?" I asked.

"Sounds good," he replied. "Are you sure you'll be okay though? The aroma of meat and seafood could be too strong for a vegetarian like you."

"I'll be okay. You must be missing meat after our vegan meal today."

"Not really," Rory said. "My roommate, Jai, hardly eats meat. And he makes delicious meatless food. So, I'm used to it. But it will be fun to explore the street food."

"Here they come."

The four of us took a bus to Tai O, a fishing village. We were fascinated by the houses on stilts in this historic town. It was a real wonder these structures were sturdy after so many years.

Next, we strolled through the street food market. People had flocked near the famous little shops to try their goodies. We stood in line in front of the most crowded store.

"Since we can't research our options, let's run with other people's opinions," Desmond rationalized, and we all agreed.

We watched the shopkeepers deep-fry a special type of donut, which they rolled in sugar.

"It looks delicious, but that's not vegetarian," Champa whispered to me. "They cook it in animal fat."

"But they have the tofu pudding you both can try," Rory said.

When it was our turn, Desmond ordered a lot of food. He got donuts, pastries filled with meat, fish cakes, marinated seafood, and a lot of different flavors of tofu pudding.

"We'll get vegetarian pan-fried noodles for you both," Desmond told Champa and me. He added with a chuckle, "Don't worry. The pudding is not your dinner."

I was touched by how much Desmond and Rory cared. They always ensured I had enough to eat. Back home, my friends called me a bother and asked me to set the meat aside and eat the rest of the dish. I'd had to remind Diego multiple times that I was vegetarian.

From the looks on the boys' faces, it was obvious their dishes were yummy. We waited for them to finish their food before digging into the dessert. We polished the pudding off within minutes. It was unbelievably delectable. Desmond had ordered so much, but our tastebuds still craved more. But it was a real pity our stomachs were full.

We ordered the takeout of veggie pan-fried noodles and headed to the metro station. We didn't get to sit in the train, as it was full. I tried not to nod off in a standing position, tired from an awesome day in Lantau Island. I couldn't wait to get home and stretch my legs. My friends looked as exhausted as me, ready to plop on their futons the minute we reached the apartment.

Back in our building, the elevators were too crowded, so we dragged ourselves up the stairs. As we walked to our apartment, we argued about who would take a shower first before dinner. We played a series of "rock, paper, scissors," to decide the bathing order.

"Hey, that's not fair," Rory complained after coming in last. "Paper is too light to overpower a mighty rock."

Champa giggled as she removed the key from her pocket when we reached the door. "Don't be a sore loser. I'm taking a shower before you."

Everyone laughed.

But our fun was short-lived as I gasped in horror. "The padlock is broken, and the door is already open. Someone was here."

The four of stood rooted in our positions, shell-shocked.

What a horrifying end to a wonderful day.

Chapter 17

Rory

When I could move again after recovering from the initial shock of learning our apartment was broken into, I rushed inside with the others. First, we checked if was anyone still there. We were relieved that it was empty but devastated to see the state of our belongings.

Our bags had been emptied and our things were strewn all over the place. Some of our stuff was wet, and we had no space to walk or stand. It was hard to figure out what was missing. After almost an hour of putting our belongings back, we had a list of items that were stolen.

The thieves had taken Champa's designer vegan leather handbag, my spare wallet, Desmond's electric shaver, my rechargeable batteries and charger, and Keira's hair dryer. Most of our clothes were gone, particularly shirts. But the worst thing was, they had stolen my credit card from my spare wallet and Champa's debit card, which had been in her handbag.

Desmond laughed humorlessly. "At least they spared our personal care products."

I shook my head. "This is a disaster."

Suddenly, Champa screamed from the kitchen. "What the heck?"

Keira rushed there and gasped. "The microwave oven and toaster are gone." She added, "And the electric kettle is broken and there are glass pieces on the floor. Be careful, the kitchen floor is still slippery."

"I'm more upset they killed the ants," Champa said, pointing to the dead insects on the kitchen floor. "Someone must have dropped the kettle filled with water on them."

"Maybe that's why the thieves spared at least some of our stuff," I reasoned. "Perhaps, they got scared that someone heard the loud noise of glass shattering on the floor and ran away."

"Champs, don't touch the glass with your bare hands," Desmond urged. "You'll get hurt."

"It's okay, I'm fine," Champa replied. "I want to check if any ants are still alive."

Champa hadn't been this upset when she discovered her expensive handbag was gone. It was fascinating how much she loved these creatures.

Keira sat down on the kitchen floor and patted Champa's back lightly to comfort her. Champa used a paper napkin to clean up the insect remains gently, being careful to keep them intact. She placed them on a plate.

She turned to us. "I'll be right back. They must be sent away respectfully. I'll return them to Mother Earth."

Keira got up. "I'm coming with you."

When Champa and Keira left, I turned toward Desmond. "What should we do next? Cancel the stolen credit and debit cards? Or buy new shirts?"

"Let's split the tasks and do both," Desmond suggested.

"Alright then, Champa and I will go to Yuan's store to cancel the cards. You and Keira can get us some new shirts."

"That's a good plan."

When the girls came back, we decided to finish cleaning up later and proceed with our plan. We used my suitcase lock for the apartment door temporarily. It could be broken easily, but we didn't have much left to steal.

Champa and I walked to Yuan's convenience store in silence, both of us preoccupied with our thoughts. I felt stupid for leaving my credit card carelessly in my suitcase while traveling. And I hadn't even locked it.

I sighed loudly, startling Champa.

"Sorry," I said.

"It's alright," Champa replied. "There's no point pondering about what happened. My mother is going to be very upset about the hand-bag. It was hers. She had given it to me very reluctantly."

"Yet you were more upset about the ants," I teased.

"I can work my behind off and replace that bag for her. But the ants are gone forever. They will never come back," Champa replied seriously. She forced a laugh. "You think I'm crazy for caring about creepy crawly creatures, don't you?"

I shook my head. "Not at all. You're right. Life is more important than materialistic things."

"Yes, *all* life is essential. I don't understand people's partial behavior. If something happens to their pet dogs or cats, they're upset. But if insects are hurt, no one cares."

"It's not that *no one* cares." I smiled and pointed at her. "You do." I added after a pause, "And thanks to you, I'll start too. I'm an avid camper, and I love animals. But I never cared about insects, reptiles, and other lesser-liked creatures until now. I can't promise I'll love them, but I'll at least try not to step on them or disturb them."

Champa grinned. "Thanks."

"And if anyone thinks you're crazy, ignore them. Because the world needs people like you."

We reached Yuan's convenience store, but we didn't see him. Only Grandpa Yu was at the cashier counter.

"He's going to lecture us again for being irresponsible teenagers," Champa whispered.

I sighed. "We have no choice though. We have to cancel our cards."

We approached Grandpa Yu, who was busy reading a magazine. Surprisingly, the shop was almost empty with only one other customer.

I knocked on the cashier counter. "Um, sir, can you please help us?"

Grandpa Yu looked up from his book. "Yes?"

"Someone broke into our apartment earlier today and stole our credit cards and debit cards," Champa explained. "Can you let us use your computer to cancel them?"

"Don't you have your phones?" Grandpa Yu asked. "I thought you must have bought new ones by now."

We shook our heads.

"Who stole your cards? Why did you keep them in the apartment? You know when I was your age, all my friends had at least one thing stolen from them. But to this date, no one could rob me. I don't let them. That's because I know the value of money, unlike you youngsters of today."

He was way out of line, but we listened without interrupting him as he went on about how today's parents fail to discipline their children. He told us a story of the time when he was in a foreign country and had cleverly escaped from muggers without losing a single cent. This man loved the sound of his own voice.

I bit my tongue hard to stop myself from laughing. Champa's attention had been diverted by the lizard on the wall behind Grandpa Yu. Unknowingly, she was imitating the animal trying to catch a fly by sticking her tongue out.

I nudged her with my elbow to stop doing that before Grandpa Yu saw her. He would give her an earful for being disrespectful if he saw her tongue sticking out.

"Champa," I hissed through my teeth when she didn't budge. "Concentrate on Grandpa Yu."

"Sorry, sir. We will be better youngsters, sir. After all, we are responsible for the future of this world, sir," Champa said, raising her voice all of a sudden.

A howl of laughter escaped my mouth, which I desperately tried to convert into a cough.

Grandpa Yu shook his head looking very displeased. "Kids of today have no manners. In my time—"

I switched off my mind as he rambled on and on about his childhood. I nodded every five seconds, pretending that I was listening. From the corner of my eye, I saw Champa was doing the same thing. The other customer had finished shopping and stood behind us for checkout.

"Sir, please help this gentleman first," I said, hoping Granpa Yu would stop talking. "We'll wait."

Champa and I headed to the store exit.

"At this rate, we'll never get to cancel our cards," Champa commented.

I laughed despite our situation. "Tell me about it."

Champa sighed. "I wish Yuan were here. I can't stand the thought of listening to another word from that old man."

"Same here. But we don't have a choice."

"I miss my smartphone," Champa wailed. "We wouldn't have had to go through this torture if we had our phones."

"True," I said. "But since we don't have it, let's wait for Yuan. I hope he comes."

"Should we ask if he'll be here tonight?" Champa asked.

I chuckled. "Only if *you* ask."

"Rock, paper, scissors," Champa challenged me. "And you lost again."

I stuck my tongue out at her and went to ask Grandpa Yu about Yuan. But to my delight, Yuan entered just then.

"Yuan," we both shouted happily.

Champa and I canceled our cards within fifteen minutes, using Yuan's smartphone. Thank goodness, the thieves hadn't used our cards yet. We signed up for new ones to be shipped to our respective addresses in Canada in two days.

"My friend has an old spare smartphone," Yuan said. "Would you like to use it? It'll definitely help you."

"Thanks, Yuan," Champa replied. "But we can't take it. The whole point of our trip was to learn to live without these devices."

"Yes, we'll get your help again if we need it," I said.

"Are you sure?" Yuan asked.

"Yes," Champa and I answered in unison though I badly wanted to say "no."

"You guys are really brave," Yuan said. "I can't imagine being without my phone or laptop for so many days. I need them for my homework, entertainment, and everything else."

"Well, people did live without them in the past," I pointed out.

"You sound like Grandpa," Yuan teased. "I'm sorry he gave you a hard time today. My father's friend called me when you both were getting scolded by Grandpa. That's why I came. I have a test tomorrow."

"We're so sorry for bothering you," Champa said. "And thanks."

"No, don't worry about it. I needed a break anyway."

"Get back to your studies, then," I told Yuan. "We'll see you later."

"What are you planning to do for breakfast tomorrow?" Yuan asked.

Champa and I looked at each other. We had no answer for that question except surviving on plain bread and cold milk.

"Why don't you come here?" Yuan suggested. "We don't have a stove, but we have a microwave oven, a toaster, and a coffee vending machine. You could also get some of our cheap meals on-the-go for lunch and dinner."

Yuan showed us their breakfast menu. They had a few vegetarian options as well. The store seemed like a good choice to eat at now that we couldn't cook in our apartment. We thanked Yuan for his suggestion and headed back home.

"It feels like we're forgetting something," I said as we walked.

"Oh shoot, we need a new lock."

Champa ran back to Yuan's convenience store. I followed her.

We bought a new padlock. This one came with a spare key. Champa attached one of them to her keychain and handed me the other. I placed it in my backpack safely.

"I don't know how we would have managed to survive this trip without Yuan," Champa stated.

I couldn't agree more. If not for Yuan's help, we wouldn't have been able to get back home safely during the storm. We wouldn't have been at ease right now, despite being robbed either.

Now I knew how people survived without their smartphones before they were invented. They relied on other people for help.

And it was not a bad thing at all.

Chapter 18

Keira

Desmond sneezed for the fifth time as we walked. "Ugh, I have no idea how this thing started. It could be the paint fumes from the building next to ours."

"Are you okay?" I asked. "Should we get some allergy medication?"

"I'll be alright," Desmond replied, sneezing again. "I've got enough medication at home." He wiped his nose with a tissue. "I hate how I'm so sensitive to almost everything. It's embarrassing."

"Don't be embarrassed. I don't think it's such a bad thing to be sensitive. Your body knows what's not good for you and protects you."

"Ah, I never saw it that way," Desmond responded, sneezing again. "That's an interesting perspective."

I smiled. "My father used to tell my mother that. She's allergic to many things. That's why she started an all-natural beauty products brand."

"Her products are genuine. I've used other so-called natural brands, and those were no good."

I nodded. "She tests new products on herself first before approving mass production." I added with a giggle, "I still can't believe the thieves didn't take any of the beauty kits. They even took our clothes."

Desmond laughed. "It *is* funny." He pointed to a sign board. "Hey look, there's a locksmith."

I sighed. "I can't believe we didn't spot it earlier. We pass by this shop practically every day. We're too reliant on our phones and online search to find stuff."

Desmond chuckled. "So true. This trip has been an eye opener." He continued. "Even if we had come to this locksmith earlier, I don't think they would have given us duplicate keys. We might have needed a Hong Kong ID and a proof of property ownership to qualify."

"Yes. And now none of that matters, because the thieves broke the lock, so we don't even need that key anymore."

Desmond and I chatted easily as we browsed the small shops on the street. Most of them were shut for the day, but we made note of them in case we needed them later. We entered a clothes store that was going to close in fifteen minutes.

It was a small shop with shirts, tees, tank tops, and sleepwear for children. The only clothes they had in our size were matching outfits for couples. Most of these had hearts on them with other cute pictures like teddy bears and kittens.

"What the heck is this?" Desmond whispered looking amused. "Champa will kill me."

"It's embarrassing," I replied biting my tongue to prevent my laughter. "And I don't think Rory will fit into any of these. But at least, they're within our budget."

Desmond showed me a set of two purple tees. Each had a white cartoon ghost holding one-half of a heart in one hand, pointing in the opposite direction with the other. If a couple stood next to each other wearing these, the ghosts on their tees would each be pointing to their partner saying, "my boo."

"This is the only one that will fit Rory," he said, trying to maintain a straight face. "The other is approximately your size."

"No way," I protested. "We can't get that."

"I have an idea," Desmond said, looking serious. "Let's wear these cheesy tees as sleepwear. No one else will see them. That way, we can wash the ones we are wearing right now, tonight, and wear them tomorrow. And tomorrow we can buy new clothes."

"Fine," I responded with a mischievous look in my eyes. "But only on one condition. You have to get the same thing in fluorescent pink."

Desmond hesitated but agreed when the shopkeeper pointed out to us that we had to hurry up, as it was almost time to close for the day. We bought the clothes and headed back home.

While waiting for Rory and Champa, we cleaned up the apartment wearing gloves to remove the remaining pieces of broken glass. I swept the kitchen, while Desmond took care of the living room. We were exhausted when we were finally done and plonked on our folded-up futons.

My stomach growled with hunger and the aroma of the veggie noodles became stronger by the minute.

"Hey, Keira, why don't you eat and go to bed? I'll wait for Champa and Rory."

I shook my head. "Thanks, but I'll wait for them. Champa must be starving too."

He handed me some cookies from his bag. "Then, eat these for now."

"Thanks."

When I was about to open the packet, Rory and Champa entered.

"All good?" Desmond asked.

"Yes," Champa answered. "All thanks to Yuan Yu."

"And not Grandpa Yu," Rory added with a laugh.

"I want to hear all about it," I said. "But first, let's eat."

We served ourselves the takeout veggie noodles and sat on the futon-couches in our living room.

"Des, are you okay to eat these cold noodles?" Champa teased. "We can't reheat them."

Desmond threw a ball of tissue paper at her. "Shut up. I'm not fussy."

Champa rolled her eyes. "Oh please. You are *very* particular about food."

"Was," Desmond responded. "This trip has changed me."

"Me as well," I said. "I've learned to appreciate the little things."

"Like the people around us," Champa added. "Especially Yuan."

"The nice lady at the café the other night who gave us free egg tarts and coffee," Rory quipped. "And Ms. Lau who served us food after her restaurant was closed."

"We should give them something as a token of our gratitude before we leave," I suggested.

"I agree," Rory replied. "But first, let's file a police report against the robbers. Maybe that can help us get our stuff back."

"It's not a good idea to contact the police," Desmond said. "We'll have to tell them the truth about Mobile Rehab and how we were conned."

Rory frowned. "What's wrong with that?"

"They might ask us why we didn't file a complaint against the Hongs in the first place," Desmond answered. "And why we're staying in this house unauthorized."

"The police might ask us to leave," Champa added. "I don't want to do that."

"Yes, and what if they contact our parents?" Desmond asked.

I didn't want the police to contact my mother. Already, I was not on good terms with her.

"Let's drop the idea of filing a police report," I said.

Rory nodded. "Alright. Let's hope nothing worse happens."

After dinner, we washed the dishes, cleaned up the mess the robbers had made, and did our laundry. Once we were done, Desmond and I handed Rory and Champa their tees for the night with poker faces. They opened the brown paper-covered clothes carefully. Both of them screamed in unison when they saw the shirts.

"What the actual f—" Champa almost swore.

"Didn't you guys get *anything* else?" a flummoxed Rory asked.

We both shook our heads.

"It was either this or nothing," I replied.

"Nothing!" Champa shouted. "Nothing would have been better."

"Relax," Desmond said, trying not to laugh. "We're wearing these now, when no one can see us. We'll save our spare stuff for tomorrow."

We showered and wore the hideous ghost tees. Rory's and my purple ones were a tad better than the fluorescent pink ones that had yellow ghosts on them. Champa and Rory covered their chests, clearly embarrassed to be seen in them. However, Desmond and I were cool about the situation.

"Picture time," I announced.

"No way," Champa shrieked.

"Over my dead body," Rory added.

"Fine, let's take one then, Keira," Desmond said. He stuck his tongue out at the other two. "You both are so snooty."

Desmond and I stood next to each other with silly grins and took a selfie. Champa pushed Desmond away playfully and clicked a picture with me. Next, I took a photo of both of them.

Rory watched us from the side, still trying to cover his shirt with his hands. His cheeks were pink like a cute kid. I wanted to pinch them.

"Come on, Rory," Champa urged.

Rory shook his head.

"We won't show these photos to anyone," Desmond said. "We promise."

Champa and I nodded in agreement.

Rory sighed. "Alright, I'll stand for one photo."

The four of us took a funny selfie. We pointed to our shirts with exaggerated grins on our faces. We looked ridiculous, but it was so much fun.

Desmond clicked a photo of Rory and Champa showing off their biceps and baring their teeth. They looked like two cute chimps ready for a fist fight.

"Now it's your turn," Champa said to Rory and me.

Rory and I stood next to each other, our legs almost touching. He made a "v" shape with his fingers and held it above my head like horns. I tried doing the same, but he was too tall. I was about to lose my balance from trying to stand on my tippy toes but caught hold of his shirt just in time.

And at that exact moment, Champa clicked the picture.

When the photo printed, it looked like I had my hand around Rory's waist, leaning close to him. It looked like we were a real couple. I felt my face getting hot and hoped no one would notice.

"If we had our smartphones, we could have taken pictures of the Polaroid photographs," Champa stated.

"I'll do that when I get home and send you copies," I replied.

The four of us chatted and laughed as we looked at all the photos from our trip so far. We had all but forgotten we'd been robbed earlier today. We'd been through a lot since we had entered this country. Hopefully, no other unpleasant surprises were in store for us.

But the important thing was we were together in this journey.

We were there for each other.

And that eased our fears a little bit.

CHAPTER 19

Rory

We lounged on the floor after our nightly self-care routine. I'd started this in middle school after my face broke out because of the chlorine in the swimming pool water. Now, it had become a habit. I was delighted that Champa and Desmond spent some time before bed on skincare, too, and learned many things from them.

Keira watched us as we applied creams and moisturizers on our faces, hands, and legs. She seemed more at ease than last night, probably because she knew we wouldn't make her do anything she didn't want. Besides, she had naturally flawless skin that I was jealous of.

I fell asleep the minute I hit my futon, exhausted from the events of the day.

Suddenly, I woke up because I heard someone cry.

"No," Desmond sobbed. "Don't go, Mama."

"Hey, are you okay?" I asked, but he didn't respond.

I realized he was talking in his sleep. Perhaps he was having a nightmare. I patted his shoulder lightly. Within minutes, he stopped speaking and snored softly. Relieved he was asleep again, I got up to drink some water and placed a bottle next to Desmond, in case he needed it later tonight.

***

When I woke up next morning, it was quarter to seven. Everyone else was up already. I freshened up and got ready to go to Yuan's store for breakfast.

"Are you carrying your spice powder mix, Champa?" I asked on our way. "I'm addicted to it."

"So am I," Keira agreed.

Champa laughed. "I'll give you both some to carry back home. I'll get you more the next time we meet."

"Just get the recipe from Champa's mother like my father did," Desmond advised. "That's the only way you'll have enough."

"I'll email it to you when I get back," Champa replied. "Keira, I hope you're carrying the catupiry cheese."

"Yes, I am," Keira confirmed.

When we reached Yuan's store, I hoped Grandpa Yu wouldn't be there. Without a cup of coffee, there was no way I would be able to bear him.

A lady greeted us with a smile. "Good morning. You must be the group Yuan spoke about. I'm his mother."

We greeted Mrs. Yu and chatted about Yuan. She told us she spent most of her time tending to Yuan's father, who was sick. That's why Yuan helped at the store more often after school these days. Mrs. Yu felt bad her eighteen-year-old son, who already had his hands full with high school exams and college entrance tests, had to manage the store in his parents' absence almost every evening. We assured her Yuan had been really helpful to us and that we were very grateful.

Mrs. Yu showed us the available breakfast options. There was the traditional Hong Kong breakfast, consisting of soup, rice or noodles, and dumplings. They also had breakfast sandwiches and boiled eggs. All the foods had a plant-based version. The vending machine had coffee, tea, herbal tea, soda, and hot chocolate.

"Choose whatever you'd like, and I'll help you check out at the counter," Mrs. Yu said.

We got our food and beverages, impressed with the variety and the reasonable prices. After paying, we sat at a table on the patio and enjoyed our breakfast.

"This isn't bad at all," Desmond commented. "I was worried it would be stale."

The rest of us nodded in agreement, our mouths full.

"So, what's the plan today?" I asked after finishing my breakfast sandwich.

"I vote for taking it easy and relaxing," Keira answered. "We had a hectic day yesterday."

"I second that," I said. "Maybe we can go somewhere nearby."

"Sorry, guys, but I have something important I need to do," Desmond said.

"I'll come with you," Champa replied.

"We won't be back until four in the afternoon," Desmond stated. "If we get delayed, we'll call this store."

"Take your time," I said. "We have a set of keys to the apartment now anyway."

"Rory, Keira, can you both buy all of us some shirts?" Champa requested.

"Make sure they aren't ridiculous like the ones we bought yesterday," Desmond added with a smile.

When we were about to leave, Mrs. Yu came to our table. "Yuan told me you got robbed yesterday. I recommend you leave your luggage in our storage lockers here and carry only what you need every evening."

"Thanks, Mrs. Yu. We'll do that," Keira responded.

Desmond gave Champa a worried look.

"We'll get your bags," I told them. "You proceed with whatever you need to do."

"Thanks, man," Desmond replied with a wide grin. "I owe you one."

After the two left, Keira and I walked back to our apartment and brought everyone's bags to the store in a cab. All our suitcases had been repacked neatly last night, so we just had to drag them to the taxi.

When we offered to pay for the storage lockers, Mrs. Yu refused. She said it was terrible we'd been robbed, and this was the least they could do for us. She also mentioned it was not a regular service. They just wanted to help us. We thanked her profusely.

"So, what should we do now?" I asked Keira. "Any ideas?"

"I have lots," Keira answered. "But it doesn't seem right to do any of those without Champa and Desmond."

"Alright, pick any one of these," I said holding up three fingers.

"What do they stand for?"

"Beach, mall, and market," I replied.

"Let's go to the beach." Keira showed me the nearest one on her map. "It's just five stops away."

I chuckled. "If we take the correct bus this time."

She laughed. "Let's check again."

We confirmed the right route from the city brochure that had most of the popular tourist spots in the city. I still missed my cell phone, which could have done the work in one-fifth of the time, but learning to use physical maps and travel brochures wasn't so bad. I hated to admit it, but they were more reliable.

We reached the beach within an hour, chatting easily during the bus journey. I was worried it would be awkward talking to Keira, but that wasn't the case. Instead of feeling nervous around her, I had a permanent smile on my face. And I had a comfortably warm and fuzzy feeling inside my chest the whole time.

I changed into my swimwear and waited for Keira, admiring the picturesque sight in front of me. The golden sand glowed under the sun, whose color was a perfect contrast to the azure ocean. The quiet waves caressed the shore gently, making me feel relaxed. I felt hypnotized by the calm sea that seemed to call out to me to embrace its crystal-clear water.

I felt my eyes welling up, as every cell in my body ached to enter the water. But I couldn't move even a single muscle as my mind filled with painful memories.

My former coach screaming at me to go faster. Him belittling me for my poor performance. My arms and legs wanting to succumb to the immense pain from practicing for hours upon hours nonstop.

Slowly, I had begun to dread swimming, something I used to love most in this world. My passion for the sport had been replaced by self-doubt. It became worse every time I failed to break a speed record, and Coach's words, "You're useless, Matthews," rang in my mind. But I hadn't given up because my passion for swimming was still alive.

But when my former coach betrayed me, I couldn't take it anymore. And I quit.

"Rory, shall we go?" Keira asked.

I turned toward her. She looked really cute in the dark-blue, skirted swimsuit with white and yellow flowers. It was hard to tear my eyes off her, but I forced myself, not wanting to make her feel self-conscious.

"Sure. After you."

Keira squealed gleefully as she ran into the water. I followed her slowly, but I didn't enter the ocean right away. I stood on the shore, letting the waves kiss my feet.

"Why are you standing so far away?" Keira called out. "Come on in. It's so nice and refreshing."

"In a moment," I answered. "I need some time."

Without any further questions, Keira splashed around as I let the feeling of the ocean sink in. At first, I took baby steps and let the water submerge my legs an inch at a time. But something finally came over me, and I involuntarily ran into the sea, took a deep breath, and jumped, enjoying the familiar wet feeling across my body.

I kicked the water and rose to the surface swaying my arms back and forth. I chuckled as a wave tried to push me, and I swam against it. It was like I was greeting every wave in this vast ocean. The force of the sea became stronger as I continued, until I realized I had swum out quite far, where it was deep.

I turned around and thrust my face out of the water. I could see the silhouette of Keira waving at me. I swam back as fast as I could, the ocean helping me this time. The salt from the sea stung my eyes, but I wasn't bothered by it. I felt a wave of joy—pun intended—like I hadn't experienced in a long time. I was like a dolphin in the water and never wanted to get out.

When I reached the shore, Keira ran toward me. "Rory, are you alright? I was so worried you were in danger."

I smiled reassuringly at her. "I'm fine. I'm a swimmer, remember?"

Uttering those words made me realize the truth in them. I *was* a swimmer. I loved swimming. I wasn't sure if I wanted to get back to races and competitions, but I knew one thing.

I would not quit swimming ever again.

CHAPTER 20

Keira

Rory plopped on the sand with a wide grin that lit up his whole face. He shook his head vigorously to get the excess water from his hair. He looked up at the sky and laughed like a child, repeating, "I'm swimming again," over and over.

I was really glad to see Rory happy. He had looked distressed standing near the shore. When he jumped into the water suddenly, I almost had a heart attack. However, when I saw him swim, I was mesmerized. He looked so graceful navigating the mighty ocean with his strong arms that I didn't notice he had gone too far.

Just when I was about to call for help, I noticed him swimming back to the shore.

I felt his fierce passion for the sport. He looked like he belonged with the water.

Like he was born to swim.

As he approached the shore, I clicked a picture of his triumphant expression with my camera. I was no professional, but this photograph had captured Rory and the scenic background beautifully. The lighting, the angle, and the clarity were all perfect.

I sat down next to Rory on the warm sand and handed him the picture. "Here you go. I took this for you."

Rory ran his finger across the photograph gingerly and smiled. "It's amazing. Thanks."

We sat in comfortable silence. I enjoyed the cool sea breeze on my face as I watched the ocean, while Rory admired his photo. I closed my eyes, a new song forming in my mind. Humming the tune, I got my notebook out and wrote it down before I forgot. I wished I had my guitar, which would have made this easier.

I had written three new songs in the last three days. This was a new record for me. Back home, it took me at least a week to compose one piece. Here, my ideas were flowing seamlessly. It was probably because I wasn't worried about my brother or my friends commenting on my creation.

"Are you writing another song?" Rory asked.

I nodded. "Yes. Was I too loud?"

"No. I wish you were, though. It was soothing."

I smiled. "When I finish it."

"Are you studying music?" Rory asked.

I sighed. "I wanted to. But my mother decided I should get a degree in accounting science. How about you?"

"I'm majoring in life sciences," Rory replied. "My entire family went to medical school. So I decided to follow them. I changed my major after trying some other things for a few months."

"Wow, you're going to be a doctor. That's hard work."

He laughed. "I haven't decided yet. But I can tolerate life sciences better than tech, literature, and other subjects."

"Same here. I'm good at accounting, but I don't particularly like it."

Rory nodded. "I get how you feel. I'm not sure if medical school is right for me. But I don't know what else to do."

I smiled. "It's so nice to meet someone who feels the same way I do. My friends know what they want to do in life. It's frustrating that I don't."

"I feel left out too," Rory said. "All my friends have clear goals as well."

I got up and brushed the excess sand off my swimsuit. "Oh well, we're still young. I'm sure we'll figure it out." I held my hand out to him. "Let's focus on having fun right now. The waves are calling us."

Rory took my hand and jumped. "Let's go."

We ran toward the ocean screaming like little kids. The wind speed had increased, and the waves were bigger now. We played and danced in the water, careful not to go too deep.

"Let's play a game," I suggested. "Whoever succeeds in making the other person fall into the water first buys lunch."

Rory grinned. "Challenge accepted." He added after thinking for a moment. "Let's have a safe word if either of us wants to back out of the game if it gets uncomfortable."

"Okay, let's use 'smart phone' as the safe word," I suggested.

"Cool. Ready? We start the game now."

Rory charged toward me to pick me up, but I ran. I splashed water on his face so that he couldn't see.

Rory laughed. "Keira, I'm a swimmer. Water won't blind me."

I had to think fast. Rory was nimble and more athletic than me. There was little chance for me to win.

He lifted me up with one of his hands under my knees and the other under my waist. He was about to throw me into the water when I shrieked. "This isn't fair. You're taller and bigger than me."

He snickered. "Sore loser."

I brought my face closer to his, one inch at a time, my heart racing. Rory's body went stiff as our eyes held each other's gaze.

Before I lost myself in those wonderful warm pools of coffee, I placed my hands on his strong shoulders and shoved with all my might. He lost his balance and fell on his back with me on top of him.

I struggled to open my eyes under the salty water. As it trickled up my nostrils and stung my insides, I realized I had forgotten to hold my breath. I forced my face out of the water and coughed.

"Are you alright?" Rory asked placing his hands on my shoulders.

"I'm fine."

"Look up," Rory said patting my back lightly. "It helps."

When I felt better, I shouted triumphantly with a fist pump in the air. "I won."

Rory rolled his eyes. "You cheated."

I stuck my tongue out at him. "You started it."

"I demand a rematch."

"Fine," I said. "Best of five."

Rory smirked. "Remember to hold your breath this time, because I'm getting revenge."

We continued the game for a few more rounds until I admitted defeat. I never won again. Rory was too fast and struck me when I was least expecting it. I was exhausted but didn't want to stop because I was having too much fun. However, when our stomachs growled with hunger, we decided to change and grab lunch.

In the changing room, I couldn't stop thinking about Rory carrying me earlier. I'd been about to put my arms around his neck while gazing into his eyes. Our faces had been dangerously close together. From our proximity, I'd heard Rory's heart pounding as fast as mine.

I had jumped into the water in an attempt to break our romantic tension...along with trying to win our game. But, for a minute, I had forgotten the bet. And from the way he looked at me, I knew Rory had too. Was our attraction mutual?

The thought of Rory having a crush on me was both exciting and scary. However, I had to work harder to keep things platonic between us. I wasn't capable of a fling and got attached too fast. Besides, I couldn't forget that I hadn't yet broken up with Diego.

I had to remember that Rory was my *friend*.

And I couldn't allow us to become more than that right now.

***

I was relieved that neither Rory nor I were awkward when we searched for a restaurant to have lunch. We wanted to eat something other than rice or noodles. After looking for almost half an hour, we found a burger joint that had a veggie option at a reasonable price.

We gobbled up our food in silence, though its taste was just okay. The burger was a little too sweet, and the fries were soggy. However, I was thankful to have a vegetarian meal that was light on the pocket. The only other place that served vegetarian food in the area was an Indian restaurant that looked expensive.

After lunch, Rory and I boarded the metro to a nearby market to buy some clothes for all of us. The market had many tiny shops on the sidewalk that sold everything from street food, to clothes, to utility items. The streets were narrow, so the place was crowded. It was a good thing vehicles weren't allowed on this road.

Rory and I wore our backpacks on the front to safeguard them from thieves. A large group of teenagers charged toward us, and I moved to the side. When they'd passed, I couldn't see Rory. There were too many people.

I stood near a café where the sign board read, "To use the bathroom or Wi-Fi, you must order." People kept shoving me aside to enter the eatery. It was the only place on the street with a prominent sign board, so I decided to wait for Rory here. If he didn't come in the next fifteen minutes, I would walk back to the metro station and wait near the entrance like we had decided.

Rory arrived five minutes later. He was trying to say something, but I couldn't hear him. He held out his hand. I took it, and we walked together as fast as we could. We stopped when we saw a small clothes store. They had souvenir tees with dragons, the beach, the Big Buddha, and other famous tourist spots. We bought a few sets for a really good discount.

Rory got some additional souvenir shirts for his family and friends. I was jealous when he went on about how much they would love the gifts. He seemed genuinely happy to go back to his loved ones.

I was dreading seeing my family and so-called friends again. Not wanting to look like a thoughtless person, I bought t-shirts with drag-ons for my brother and my mother. But I wasn't sure if I'd ever give them the presents.

When we exited the shop, it was eating me up that Rory bought six additional tees when I only got two. Hesitantly. Did I really have no one in my life? Suddenly, I missed my father. He would have loved this souvenir shop. I would have gotten him more than one shirt, a cap, and maybe a few different keychains and fridge magnets.

My eyes brimmed with tears, but I blinked them away. Rory called out my name, but I was too embarrassed to look at him. I didn't want him to see me cry. Discreetly, I wiped my eyes on my sleeve. However, Rory noticed.

"Are you okay?"

"Something got in my eye," I lied.

He let go of my hand and stood in front of me. "Do you want me to look?"

I shook my head. "Thanks, but let's find a less-crowded area."

"I agree. This place is making me claustrophobic."

We held hands again and strode faster, almost running.

"Hey, look." I pointed to a brick red building with large glass windows. "I know that place. Let's go there."

The bar was almost empty, with only one other table with people. It was dimly lit, and an old English song played softly in the background. The antique furniture looked like it was from the Victorian era. Framed photos of British generals and royals hung on the walls. Toward the side was a large grandfather clock that occupied most of the space in this cozy pub.

"Can I see your IDs, please?" the server requested. He checked them and handed them back. "Would you like a table? You can also sit on the bar stools near the counter."

"We'd prefer a table please," I answered looking at Rory, who held a thumbs-up.

"I'll give you some time to decide your order," the server said and left.

Rory had a confused expression on his face.

"I know you don't drink." I rummaged through my backpack and took out an envelope carefully. I opened it and showed him a photo. "My father and his friends came here. See, they took this picture in front of this building."

Rory pointed at one of the people in the photograph. "This is him, correct? You resemble him a lot."

I nodded and grinned widely. "Thanks." I showed him another one. "And he clicked this solo inside."

"We're sitting at the same table."

I squealed. "Really? We should take a picture of me. Wait, let me get the same beer."

I ordered the beer for me and a soda for Rory. While we waited for our drinks, I showed him the rest of the photos.

"This one of Pai's—my father's—favorite photographs," I said, showing him a pic of my father and his friends in front of the Big Buddha.

"We have one now too," Rory pointed out. "The four of us took one in the same place, right?"

I nodded. "Yes. I wanted to go everywhere my father went to feel closer to him."

Rory placed his hand on mine. "Let's do that. Let's go to all those places."

"Thanks. But I don't think we can go to Victoria Peak. It's out of our current budget."

"True," Rory replied. "Maybe the four of us can come back in a few years. Or perhaps your father will create a miracle for us to visit this time."

I laughed. "You think so?"

"Well, you never know. I believe it's your father looking out for us."

I wanted to get up and hug Rory for saying that. Instead, I reached out and took both his hands in mine.

"Thanks. That's really sweet of you. I don't usually talk about my father. But I'm glad I shared these with you."

Rory beamed at me and squeezed my hands. "I miss my grandfather too. My mother's father. I was very close to him." He added after a pause. "He died because of alcohol poisoning. That's why I don't drink. Very few people know this."

"I'm sorry for your loss, Rory. And I'm sure your grandfather is with my father, looking after us."

He smiled and nodded. "Thanks."

After showing Rory the rest of the photographs, I placed them back in my bag. Just then, our drinks arrived, and we clinked our glasses and said, "cheers" before taking a swig. I closed my eyes, feeling the cold beer chill my insides.

"Whoa," Rory exclaimed. "This is really cold."

"Yes, I could almost feel my brain freeze." I placed my glass aside. "Anyway, can you show me your sketch books if you're okay with it?"

"Sure. I have one condition, though. You're not allowed to touch them."

I agreed, and Rory showed me his drawings. They were really good. I liked the dinosaur and the scenery sketches in the pocket notebook. But my favorite one was that of the Buddha in the big book.

"Wow. This is amazing. It looks very similar to the actual sculpture."

"It's not that good," Rory replied modestly. "I'm just a beginner."

Rory closed the book. I noticed he didn't show me the last sketch.

"There was one more drawing in your book. Aren't you going to show it to me?"

Rory placed his sketchbook back in his bag, trying to hide his face. But that was only making his blush more obvious. "That's a secret."

I didn't press him further, but I was really curious to see that last sketch. Did it have anything to do with me?

I badly wanted to snatch the book back from his backpack and sneak a peek. But I didn't. Partly because it would be rude to do that.

But also because I was scared my hunch that it had something to do with me was right.

And what if it wasn't?

Honestly, I didn't know which was worse.

CHAPTER 21

Rory

Keira looked like she was about to snatch my bag and look at the drawing I didn't show her. So I placed it deep inside my backpack. I looked at her from the corner of my eye when I hid my flushed face. Her cheeks had turned pink too. Did she guess that I had sketched her? Well, she would never find out.

If I had shown her the drawing, I'd have made my crush on her more obvious. She probably knew all about it. When she had brought her face really close to mine and I had lost my balance, I hadn't fallen because she shoved me. I had fallen because she caught me off guard with her proximity.

But did she really come close to kissing me just to win the game or was the attraction from both sides? From the look on her face right now, I was pretty sure it was the latter.

I slowly raised my head, composing myself, and took another sip of my soda.

Though I was glad our crush was mutual, I knew neither of us would cross any lines, because if that happened, we would feel guilty and remorseful, instead of being here together now—sharing parts of ourselves we didn't normally talk about.

Honestly, I preferred this.

"So, do you have a lot of friends?" Keira asked. "You bought quite a few souvenirs earlier. I'm kind of jealous."

"Well, of the six shirts I got, three are for my friends," I answered. "The rest are for my family."

"That's still three more friends than I have left," Keira murmured, but I heard her.

"Friendship is a touchy topic for me as well." I took a long sip of my soda and chuckled humorlessly. "My life was turned upside down overnight because of some fake ones. And it hurt like crazy, though I deserved it. You see, I was a terrible friend too."

"Whoa. That sounds intense."

I nodded. "The three friends I have right now are good people. I trust them with my life. But I can't *trust* them. Do you know what I mean?"

Keira shook her head. "I don't get that at all. But I'm intrigued."

"If my life was in danger, I know for sure that my three friends would save me," I explained. "But..." I trailed off, scared that Keira might judge me. I was being too vulnerable right now, and I hadn't even had a single drop of alcohol.

"But?" Keira prompted me. She added after a pause, "It's okay if you don't want to talk about it."

There was no judgment or pity in Keira's eyes. She seemed genuinely interested in hearing me out. Besides, she had trusted me not to judge her when she shared about her friends. And if she did think less of me after this conversation, I wouldn't have to care much, because I would probably never see her again after this trip.

I took a deep breath. "But I can't trust them not to leave me alone again."

Keira took my hands in hers. "I'm sorry. That must have been awful for you."

"It was. Though I deserved it."

"Why do you feel that way? Did you mean to hurt them?"

I shook my head. "No. In fact, I thought I was protecting my best friend from the fake people's toxicity by staying silent. But I realized too late that I had hurt her by not standing up for her."

"I'm sure she'll forgive you."

"She already has," I said. "But our friendship isn't the same. And I don't know if it will ever be."

"Why not?"

"Because my best friend is hurting so much that she's failing to see *my* pain," I blurted. "She's forgiven me, yes. But she hasn't attempted to understand or empathize with me. Does she know how many times I shed tears because of those fake people?" I answered my own question. "No, she doesn't. And I haven't told her, because my petty feelings are nothing compared to what she went through because of those idiots." I sighed. "I know I sound selfish, but I really wish she would try to see my perspective at least once. Am I asking for too much?"

"No," Keira replied. "I don't think your expectation is unreasonable at all. It's natural to want to be understood. Especially by your best friend." She added after a pause, "Also, your feelings are not petty. I don't know your friend's story. But your problems are not smaller than hers or vice versa. It's not a competition."

"Thanks for listening," I said. "It's been a while since I had such a deep conversation."

Keira smiled. "No worries. I just did the same thing you did for me. Remember I told you that absurd story about my friend? That *friend* was me." She added with a smile, "Which you already knew but pretended you didn't."

I chuckled. "You're right. I knew. But that story wasn't absurd. Like you said, your feelings are valid. No one has the right to judge, measure, or compare them."

"You learn fast, Rory Matthews."

I drank the last of my soda. "I learn only from the best."

I was disappointed when we finished our drinks. I didn't want to end this conversation. The only other person I could talk to about my innermost feelings was my best friend, Tina. But we hadn't done that in a while.

"Do you want to get another drink?" Keira asked as if she read my mind. "I don't feel like getting up yet."

"Looks like you're enjoying my company too much, Keira Delgado."

"Speak for yourself, Rory Matthews." She winked at me. "I'm addictive. You'll miss me a lot later."

I was bewitched by Keira's response and couldn't say a word. She laughed, asking me again if I wanted another soda. I could only nod my head mutely.

When Keira went to the counter to order our drinks, her words rang in my head: "Your feelings are not petty." That comforted me more than any advice or suggestions. I expected her to tell me to talk it out with Tina. But she didn't. I was grateful for that. It made me trust her.

"Here you go," Keira said, placing another soda in front of me.

"Thanks." I pointed to her drink. "You got a soda, too?"

Keira nodded. "Yeah. That beer tasted too strong. I prefer sweeter cocktails." She sipped her drink and frowned. "What *is* this? It's worse than the beer."

I laughed. "I didn't like it either."

"Then why did you get another one?"

I raised one of my eyebrows. "You tell me."

"You could have warned me."

The truth was, I hadn't paid attention to the soda at all earlier. I was too engrossed in our conversation.

"I can't stop thinking about everything you told me about your best friend and the fake people," Keira said. "You were really cryptic, and now I'm super curious."

"Regarding my best friend, it's not my secret to spill," I replied. "However, sometime in the future, I'll tell you how the fake people tried to ruin my life. I'm not yet ready to talk about it."

"Do you plan to stay in touch with me after this trip?"

I leaned forward and looked Keira in the eyes. "Why? Do you not want to?"

"We'll see."

I enjoyed the flustered look on her face. Well, she had done the same thing to me earlier at the beach. *Two can play at this game, Keira.*

"You know, I've tried to picture being alone on this trip like I had originally planned," Keira said. "But I can't even imagine it. I've gotten used to the three of you."

"I know what you mean. There were times when I thought I should have never come here, but now, thanks to you, Desmond, and Champa, I'm really glad I did."

"I felt lonely when I got here," Keira said, her voice breaking a little. "Not a single person was on my side. That's why I came to the place where my father had found a new purpose to his life." She inhaled deeply. "Pai came here with his friends just before he divorced my mother. His relationship and career as a singer had hit rock bottom. This trip resurrected him. It helped him start over." She laughed. "He called it his 'Phoenix Holiday.' Anyway, when he came back, he was a different person. Despite separating from my mother, he was more cheerful and optimistic. He managed to regain almost all the success he had lost within the next three years. But fate was cruel to him, and he passed away in a road accident on his way to sign his biggest record deal."

"I'm so sorry to hear that, Keira."

"Thank you. For helping me see he's still taking care of me. He gave me you three. I think I finally have the courage to face the people back home now."

I reached out and squeezed Keira's hands.

She laughed. "Sorry, that got a little intense. I don't know what it is about this place. It's making both of us let out our innermost feelings."

"It's not this pub. It's us. We've kept everything bottled up for too long."

Keira nodded. "You're right. I can't remember the last time I talked like this either. Every time I tried, my boyf—, *ex*-boyfriend, made fun of me."

"The term they use is emotional availability," I stated. "Some of us need a higher level of emotional availability than others. Many call this boring, but it's our need."

"Oh, they only say it's boring when it's about you," Keira replied. "Not when it's about themselves."

I sighed. "Exactly. My ex dumped all her nonsense on me. But when I tried to talk, she belittled me."

"Mine was on his phone during *our* dates."

"Mine wanted everything her way," I said. "If I declined, she would make my life miserable."

"Make your life miserable how?"

I shuddered at the memory of Harriet's toxicity. "She'd ghost me but deny it when I asked her the reason. She'd blame me for every bad thing in her life. She'd control me to the point of suffocation. If I tried to counter her, she'd use my guilt against me."

Keira gasped. "I'm so sorry you went through that."

"Aren't you going to ask me why I put up with it for so long?"

Keira sighed and shook her head. "No, I get it. I, too, put up with Diego, my ex, for too long. I should have ended it when he disregarded my emotions and belittled me for them. But I couldn't break things off with him because of our band and mutual friends. Besides, no one believed me when I told them he was disrespectful to me, because he treated me so well in front of everyone, particularly my mother." She took a deep breath. "When we started our band, we decided we'd take turns being the lead singer. However, my brother, Sebastian, and his girlfriend, Marina, would always take the lead, never giving me a chance. I put up with this for many months, but one day I confronted them during weekend practice in our basement. During the argument, Diego put an arm around me and took me aside. I thought he understood my feelings, but later, when no one was around, he accused me of overreacting and trying to break up our band. The next day, when I talked to my mother, who had witnessed Diego's so-called supportive behavior about this incident, she took his side. She also said I should stop being so emotional and become stronger."

I felt terrible that Keira had been through the same pain as me. But it was also comforting at least one person understood me. We continued talking about our most toxic experiences. As we poured our hearts out, we realized how much these abusers had affected us.

They were wounds that only we could see, and pain that only we understood.

"I went to a therapist for panic attacks," Keira shared. "I started getting them after my father left us. Therapy helped me get better. But, back then, I didn't realize Diego was also emotionally abusing me. Now that I think about it, he was a cause for my distress too."

"I understand what you mean," I replied. "No one else knows this, but I get panic attacks too," I revealed quietly. "I didn't tell anyone because I was scared they'd call me a weakling."

Keira interlocked her fingers with mine. "Repeat after me. We are *not* weak. Nor are we stupid."

My heart started racing again when I realized that Keira and I had been holding hands this whole time. Our intertwined fingers made things feel dangerously more intimate than our physical proximity on the beach earlier.

This was not just a crush anymore.

It was much more than that.

But there was no need for any labels.

Chapter 22

Keira

Rory and I chatted in the bar for more than three hours. We finally left when people started coming inside and we realized how late it was. However, when we reached our apartment, Desmond and Champa still weren't back yet.

"Didn't Desmond say they'd be back by four?" I asked.

"Maybe they're just late," Rory replied. "Let's wait for them and go for dinner together."

"Okay, it's just half past six anyway."

We freshened up and did the laundry, including washing the new shirts we got from the market today.

When it was past eight, Champa and Desmond were still not back.

"Let's go to Yuan's store," Rory suggested. "Maybe Desmond left a message for us."

Grandpa Yu was at the store. Thank goodness it was crowded. He didn't talk to us for too long. After his usual "youngster-dissing speech," we asked him if Desmond or Champa had left us a message. But they hadn't.

Rory and I sat at the store's little table and had instant noodles for dinner. We couldn't stomach anything else because we were worried about our friends. Where were they? Why hadn't they called Yuan's store like we had decided?

"I really wish we had our mobile phones right now," I said. "At least we could have contacted them." I placed my fork in the noodle bowl. "Why don't we try Yuan's mobile number? Maybe he knows where they are."

"Great idea." Rory handed me his notebook with Yuan's number in it. "Here you go."

We called Yuan from the store phone, but he didn't pick up. We didn't leave him a voicemail because we didn't want to worry him.

"We can't even text him," I said, frustrated. "This really sucks."

We finished our dinner in silence, annoyed with the situation. Why did our wonderful days have to end so horribly?

Rory looked more upset than me, but he didn't seem to want to talk about it. So I didn't press him. I knew he'd tell me when he was ready.

I tried not to let pessimistic thoughts about Desmond and Champa cloud my mind. I hoped and prayed they were alright. I attempted to distract myself, but it was almost impossible. After all, as the older adults in the group, we felt responsible for the two seventeen-year-old minors.

"It's my fault Champa and Desmond haven't left us a message," Rory said. "I shouldn't have refused Yuan's offer to give us his friend's old smartphone."

I placed my hand lightly on his shoulder. "Don't be harsh on yourself. Champa also wanted to stay away from smartphones. All four of us did."

"But Desmond and Champa needed it badly," Rory replied, raising his voice slightly. "I should have convinced them to take the phone from Yuan."

"Don't blame yourself. I'm sure they're fine."

Though I said those words to him, I wasn't sure about them. I was only trying to comfort Rory...and myself. But I knew I didn't sound convincing.

"Should we go look for them?" Rory asked.

"Where do we go?"

Rory shrugged. "I don't know. But we can't sit idle, right? They found us when we were lost in the storm."

"They had some clues during that time," I said. "We have none."

Though I didn't want to admit it, we really were helpless this time. It wasn't safe, or wise, to go on a wild goose chase in search of our friends.

Rory got up from his seat. "Let's go back home and wait for them. We'll get something for them, in case they haven't yet eaten."

When Rory got our friends' dinner, I bought a pack each of playing cards and Uno. We had to pass the time tonight while waiting for Desmond and Champa. Before we left, we took our clothes for tomorrow from our suitcases. Since they weren't here, we decided to take our friends' luggage back home.

The other two were still not home when we reached the apartment. We changed into our ridiculous sleepwear, but unlike yesterday, it didn't make us laugh.

"Would you like to pretend we have a smartphone again?" Rory asked. "I want to mindlessly scroll some short videos."

"I don't think that'll help today." I waved the packs of cards in front of him. "How about a few games instead?"

Rory and I spent the entire night playing cards and Uno. At first, we were only trying to pass the time, but when the games got competitive, we almost forgot about Desmond and Champa's absence.

"Hey, that's not fair," Rory cried. "You can't bring a 'draw four' card at the last moment."

"Says who?" I smacked the card on top of his measly one full force. "And Uno. I win. *Again*."

"Let's play something else," Rory said, sulking. "You've rigged the Uno cards."

I laughed. "I didn't say that to you when you won every card game."

"That's because I'm not a cheater like you."

Suddenly, we heard a knock on the door. I checked through the peep hole to see if it was our friends. It wasn't. Some drunk people were causing a ruckus outside.

When they banged on the door again, Rory and I stood hand in hand, armed with a broom stick and a mop, in case they broke it down. We had the latch fastened from inside, but we were scared it might not be strong enough to protect us.

Finally, the sounds stopped, and we went back to the living room. It was past four in the morning, but there was still no sign of Champa or Desmond.

I yawned sleepily. "I can't keep my eyes open any longer."

"Me neither."

"Why don't we take a nap?" I suggested. "We can keep the lights on."

"Okay, but if the two are not back by nine in the morning tomorrow, we're contacting the police."

I agreed. Rory went to the boys' room, and I plonked on my futon in the living room. I prayed for the wellbeing of my friends one more time before I drifted off to sleep.

***

I woke up to Desmond and Champa whispering near the entrance. I got up with the jolt.

"Where the heck were you two?" I shouted, forgetting Rory might still be asleep, but he came rushing out of his room. "Do you know how worried we both were?"

"We left you a message with Grandpa Yu," Desmond said, looking genuinely surprised at our anger. "Didn't he relay it to you?"

"We were with Desmond's family," Champa explained. "They asked us to spend the night."

"We're really sorry we worried you," Desmond added. "But Grandpa Yu promised he would let you know."

Rory and I looked at each other and mouthed, "what the heck?" We were furious that we had needlessly stayed up the whole night, anxious about our friends. If Grandpa Yu had just told us our friends were alright, Rory and I could have relaxed and enjoyed a cozy evening in our apartment.

I felt the blood rush to my face. What was I thinking? I would have been anything but relaxed.

If all was well, Rory and I wouldn't have been comfortable being alone together in the apartment. In our current "mutual attraction" situation, it would have been easy to cross the boundary that was already thinning between us.

It's not like I didn't trust myself, but still...

"Keira, are you okay?" Champa asked.

"Y—Yeah, I'm fine." I faked a yawn. "I'm still a little groggy. That's all."

"Let's sleep for a while," Champa said. "It's just half past five."

When I woke up, it was almost noon. The other three were up and ready for lunch. I brushed my teeth and threw on a pair of jeans and the dragon souvenir shirt as fast as I could.

"We're getting waffles today," Desmond announced. "It's my treat."

"That sounds yum," Rory replied. "But first, let's go to Yuan's store and have a chat with Grandpa Yu."

At the store, we asked Yuan's grandfather if he remembered Desmond and Champa calling. He got angry with us for doubting him and gave us an earful. When we were about to leave, Mrs. Yu appeared.

"I'm sorry for the confusion yesterday," she said. She showed us a handwritten note with Desmond's and Champa's message. "Yuan's grandfather must have forgotten about this. He's losing his memory more often these days. It wasn't deliberate."

"Please don't apologize," Desmond replied, looking embarrassed. "It's our fault. We should have informed Yuan instead of Grandpa Yu."

"No, it was *our* mistake," Mrs. Yu insisted. "As a token of our apology, please accept these free passes to our store's tenth anniversary event at Victoria Peak next week."

The four of us looked at each other. Though we badly wanted to visit the famous Victoria Peak, accepting these expensive passes didn't seem right.

"Please don't say no," Mrs. Yu said. "We really want you to come and celebrate with us."

Champa took the passes from Mrs. Yu. "Alright, but only if you let us help you."

Mrs. Yu agreed and told us she'd give us more details soon. The event was next week, so we still had time.

When we left the store and Mrs. Yu was out of earshot, Champa and I squealed delightfully. "We're going to Victoria Peak."

Rory smiled at me secretly and mouthed, "See, I told you."

I beamed at him, mouthing back, "It's a miracle."

There was a long line outside the waffle cart. The sweet aroma of the breakfast treat made me hungrier. Champa reached into her bag and passed us each a packet of mixed nuts. We munched on those as we waited for forty-five minutes.

When it was finally our turn, Desmond ordered four large gai daan zai, or bubble waffles, for us. I got a plain waffle with raspberries and crunchy roasted peanuts. Champa got a chocolate banana one with condensed milk. And the guys each got a strawberry nut waffle.

I gorged on my gai daan zai, though it was piping hot. It was crispy on the outside but fluffy near the air pockets. The waffle had absorbed the honey and raspberry compote, making it juicy and succulent. This was definitely one of the best meals I had eaten. I could see the others agreed with me by the way they were gobbling up theirs.

"I don't want to eat ever again," Desmond finally announced, dramatically tapping his tummy.

Champa rolled her eyes. "You say that after every meal. But you're the first one who gets hungry again."

We all laughed.

"But I really can't walk now," I said. "Let's go home and take a nap."

"Absolutely not," Rory countered. "After this heavy meal, we should walk. Only then we can digest it."

The three of us made a face at Rory, but we followed him anyway. We walked aimlessly on the sidewalk one behind the other. There was no room to walk together. Sometimes small cart shops or pop-up stores were on the pavement, forcing us to walk on the main road amidst traffic. It was scary.

We saw a park with an empty playground and decided to go there. Desmond wanted to tell us something. The children's play area had a swing, a slide, two seesaws, and monkey bars. It was currently empty.

The four of us climbed up the bars and sat on the top. It was a perfect place to have a conversation. We also had a nice view of the city from there.

"I finally saw my mother yesterday, after four years," Desmond said. "She left home without a word when I was thirteen. I learned she was in Hong Kong and came here to find her. The Mobile Rehab was only a means of getting economical accommodation."

"How did you learn she was here?" I asked.

"Apparently, some reporters spotted my mother in a monastery in the background in a vlogger's video," Desmond answered. "And my mother's security team found this before the reporters made the news public. Anyway, it was supposed to be a secret, but my mother's executive assistant told me because she felt sorry for me. I used to spend a ton of time and effort looking for my mother."

"And how did you find her in Hong Kong?" Rory asked.

"I was lucky I found the vlogger's other videos about Hong Kong's monasteries, and many of them had my mother in the background. After watching them, I guessed she went to Ten Thousand Buddhas on some weekdays and Big Buddha during the weekend. I finally saw her today in Ten Thousand Buddhas."

Wow. Desmond's story was like a novel.

I'd only read crime stories where the police searched for the criminal in the backgrounds of photos and videos. Seeing a real-life example was baffling, to say the least.

"Is your mother alright?" Rory asked.

Desmond nodded. "She's doing better now."

"Was she ill?" I asked.

"She told me she needed time for herself," Desmond answered. "That's why she left home."

"She wanted to take care of her mental and emotional wellbeing, away from prying eyes," Champa explained. "She was the CEO of a well-known conglomerate and couldn't afford to ruin her reputation."

"My mother is staying with her parents in my grandparents' holiday home in Hong Kong," Desmond added. "I had no clue they had a house here."

"Are *you* okay, Desmond?" I asked.

"I don't know," Desmond replied. "It's hard to explain how I'm feeling. I'm relieved she's okay but also upset she left without saying a word to me. And didn't try to get in touch with me all this time."

"We're okay if you want to spend more time with your family," Rory said. "Don't hold back for us."

"Um, my family thinks we're in Hong Kong on our school trip," Desmond replied. "So does Champa's."

"And our classmates don't know we're here either," Champa added. "They didn't want us to go with them on the school trip."

Rory frowned. "What do you mean by that? Did your classmates say they didn't want you around?"

Desmond shook his head. "No, but it was obvious. No one wanted to room with us or discuss the trip with us. They'd suddenly stop talking when we were in the room and make faces. I told you we're outcasts."

"So, we lied to everybody," Champa said. "We told our teachers we were staying back to prepare for our upcoming tournaments to excuse ourselves from the trip."

Desmond laughed. "Our teachers never question a student's schoolwork. Whether it's academics or extracurricular activities, schoolwork comes first, according to them. And the school trip wasn't compulsory, anyway. So they let us stay back."

"Yes, and we didn't want to worry our parents, so we never told them we weren't going on the school trip," Champa continued. "My parents sort of know I'm not liked at school, unlike my popular sister, but they'd be too hurt if they learned I'm an outcast."

"My poor father is already stressed because of my mother," Desmond said. "I didn't want to add my problems to it."

"I'm really sorry you went through this," I said, patting Champa and Desmond lightly. "Is there anything we can do to help you feel better?"

"Let's explore every nook and cranny of this city while we're here," Desmond suggested. "That'll make me feel better. What say?"

"I'm in," I said.

"Me too," Rory echoed.

Champa clapped delightfully. "Okay, then, where do we go first?"

We planned our itinerary for the next few days, all set to explore Hong Kong on a tight budget. So, all the theme parks and other expensive areas were off limits. Champa insisted on setting some time aside to make presents for the people that helped us in this city.

When our final plan was complete, it looked perfect.

Provided everything went according to it.

Just this time, maybe it would.

CHAPTER 23

Rory

The four of us had the best time of our lives over the next few days. We visited beaches, markets, and many other tourist spots in the city. We took the hop-on hop-off day tour in the downtown area. Our favorite place was the night promenade, which had breathtaking views of Hong Kong's waterfront and skyline. My camera ran out of battery because of the number of pictures I took there.

As decided, Desmond, Keira, and I went back to the Ten Thousand Buddhas Monastery and spent an entire day there. Champa drove us all out of the apartment that day because she wanted to be alone to start working on the presents.

She went to the thrift store in our neighborhood and bought some old wooden coasters to redesign them. When we returned from the monastery, we helped Champa finish making the gifts. She had created personalized coasters with their names on them for the three businesses: Yuan's convenience store, the café where Keira and I stayed during the storm, and Mrs. Lau's restaurant, where we ate dinner after closing time on our first day here. We also made one for the hotel downstairs for lending us their carpentry tools for free.

We learned to sand and polish wooden pieces from Champa. She was an impatient teacher, though, and tough if we didn't complete the task correctly. She made us redo it until we got it right.

So Keira and I went to Desmond when we had questions. He had gotten used to his best friend's perfectionism and coordinated our team.

Once we were done, we gave the coasters to all four businesses, and they loved them, particularly Mrs. Lau, who got emotional. She thanked us for the thoughtful present and treated us to a free meal.

In just a few days, I had gotten closer to Keira, Desmond, and Champa than I had with anyone else before. I was going to miss them when this trip ended. There were four more days, but I knew those would fly by. We promised to stay in touch, but it wouldn't be the same.

Another place we would remember every time we thought of this city was Yuan's convenience store. We had lost count of the number of times we went there. We had become friends with the Yu family. Even Grandpa Yu was slowly warming up to us. At least, he stopped scowling at us when we visited and said hello.

"So, tomorrow is the big day," Mrs. Yu said during our meeting at the store a day prior to the anniversary event. "Are you all ready?"

The four of us replied in unison, "Yes!"

"Great, our shuttle will pick you up from your place at seven in the morning," Mrs. Yu told us. "Be downstairs ten minutes earlier."

We made a note of all our tasks and headed back to our apartment.

***

The next day, we reached the venue, Victoria Peak, per schedule. We'd eaten breakfast on the way and were geared up to work hard. However, Mrs. Yu urged us to see the museum and enjoy the tram ride to the Sky Terrace.

We were lucky to get a clear view of Hong Kong, as it was sunny with very few clouds in the sky. We saw a unique combination of lush greenery, giant skyscrapers, and turquoise blue water as we went up. We welcomed the cool breeze that soothed us on this warm day.

When we reached the entrance, we scanned our passes and went up the elevator to the Sky Terrace. We took as many pictures of the city as possible from the top before it got cloudy. It was quite early in the morning, but still, the terrace was crowded because many tourists were placing locks with their loved ones' names for good luck and longevity of their relationship.

"How about we place a lock with our four names?" Champa suggested.

"There are too many people right now," Desmond complained. "Do we still want to do that?"

"I don't mind," I said.

"Let's come back later then," Keira said. "We have to get to the event venue now."

The event venue was inside a huge shopping center within the Peak building. The mall had an arcade, numerous shops, interactive galleries, photo booths, and scores of other things to do. There was something for everyone. We could spend the entire day here and not get bored.

"Am I a bad person for regretting our offer to work in exchange for the free passes to the Peak?" Keira whispered to me.

"Not at all. I feel the same way."

We laughed and high-fived each other.

Keira and I always found opportunities to share private jokes with each other. We communicated with discreet eye contact and facial expressions that no one else understood. We had become experts at silently mouthing at each other when around others. The four of us were close, but what Keira and I had was special.

***

We spent until lunch helping with the event setup. There was a lot to do: arranging chairs, decorating the venue, putting up the sign boards, helping the performers, and much more. By the time we were done, we were exhausted.

When we were taking a short break, Yuan came running to us. "Can any of you sing or play an instrument? The band we hired canceled at the last minute."

I looked at Keira to see if she wanted to volunteer, but she had already raised her hand. "I'll do it."

Yuan's tense expression instantly changed into a wide grin. "Thanks, Keira. We owe you a big one."

"I don't have a guitar though," Keira said. "Can you arrange one?"

Yuan nodded. "Of course. I'll be right back." He handed us a paper bag each. "Eat something before the event."

The four of us grabbed a seat in the mall's food court and had our meal watching the news on the large wall-mounted flat screen TV.

"It's unbelievable," Desmond exclaimed. "How could the scammers sell fake pain removal cream for two years without getting caught? Didn't anyone report them?"

"The same way the Hongs have been running the viral Mobile Rehab for over a year without getting caught," Champa replied.

"You heard it yourself on the news," I said. "Every time someone posted a negative review online, it was automatically deleted. And there was no way to contact the sellers of the fake product."

"And people kept buying the pain removal cream because of the false online reviews," Keira added.

I facepalmed. "Like I did. I was attracted to the Mobile Rehab because of the raving reviews and the amazing ad."

"Well, we learned our lesson," Champa said. "All that shines is not gold."

Keira sighed. "It's going to be very hard for me to trust any seller, even if they seem genuine."

Everyone nodded in agreement in unison.

"Anyway, did you realize that that's the first screen we've seen in almost two weeks?" Champa asked. "My eyes feel weird."

Suddenly, Desmond got up from his chair and ran toward a man wearing a suit. He spoke to the man for a few minutes and stomped off angrily. We couldn't hear their conversation.

We had never seen Desmond lose his temper. Champa went after him, but she couldn't see him anymore. She went and spoke with the man who'd angered Desmond before coming back to our table.

"That's Des's father," Champa said. "He's here for a conference."

Champa didn't reveal details about anything concerning Desmond, so we didn't press her. We ate our food in silence. I noticed Keira's veggie wrap was smaller than ours. Before I could ask her if she wanted anything more to eat, Yuan arrived with her guitar.

"Here you go. Is this alright?" Yuan asked her, handing her the case.

Keira opened it and looked at the instrument. "This should work."

Yuan smiled, looking relieved. "Cool. Let's head to the dressing room then." He gave her a purse. "And this is some makeup from my mother. It's a small token of appreciation for saving the day."

"Thanks," Keira said, looking uncomfortable, probably at being gifted makeup. She got up from her seat. "But you didn't have to get me anything."

Champa followed Keira. "Let me help you get ready."

I went back to the event hall, glad to see Desmond in the front row. He had reserved seats for Champa and me.

"Where's Champa?" Desmond asked.

"With Keira."

Desmond nodded. "Cool."

"There's still time for the event to start," I said. "Let's grab something for you to eat."

Desmond shook his head. "I'm not hungry, thanks."

I noticed a scratch on Desmond's hand. It was bleeding. "Hey, you need to get that wound checked."

"It's alright. I'm fine."

I gave him a wad of paper napkins from my pocket. "Use this to stop the bleeding then."

"Thanks," he said.

"No problem. How did you get hurt?"

"The bathroom door had a nail sticking out," Desmond replied. "I scratched my hand against it."

"Have you got a tetanus shot recently?" I asked.

"Nope."

"Let's get one after this event," I said.

Desmond nodded. "Okay. Um, about earlier..."

"You don't have to explain yourself."

Desmond smiled genuinely. "Thanks."

CHAPTER 24

Keira

In the dressing room backstage, I watched Champa nervously as she examined the makeup products Mrs. Yu had gotten me. Back home, Marina did my makeup when we had a performance, and she insisted on making me look like a completely different person, because the natural me was too "ordinary." I expected Champa to transform me as well.

I clenched my teeth and closed my eyes, trying to endure the feeling of foreign products on my face.

"Relax," Champa whispered. "You'll be ready in no time."

When I opened my eyes, I was pleasantly surprised to see my face in the mirror. It didn't look much different from earlier, but it was glowing. It didn't feel heavy or uncomfortable either.

"How is it?" Champa asked. She admired my face from a distance. "You look fantastic. I didn't have to do much. I just enhanced your natural beauty."

Overwhelmed, I nodded without saying anything. I was scared I'd start crying and ruin her efforts.

"For your lips, which one do you want?" Champa asked, showing me three products. "Lip gloss, lipstick, or lip tint?"

I gave her a blank look, having no idea what the difference between the three was. Back home, Marina insisted on applying a thick coat of bright-colored lipstick that made me look like a buffoon. I hated it.

If makeup could make me look like this, though, I wouldn't dislike it so much.

"You can go with a simple lip balm, if that's what you like," Champa said, trying to help me. "What matters is that *you're* comfortable."

"Can we try and see what suits the best?" I asked.

"Of course," Champa replied. "Trials definitely help." She gently applied the three products on the back of my hand. "Which do you like the most?"

I chose the shiny lip gloss, and Champa applied it carefully on my lips with a brush.

"Try singing now," she instructed. "Is it too sticky? Should we wipe some of it off?"

I loved how caring Champa was. I had never experienced that before. Those who touched my face usually only found fault with it. They never cared about what I wanted or how I felt.

"It's perfect as it is," I said. I got up from the chair. "Can I hug you?"

Champa pulled me into an embrace. "Of course. But let's be careful not to smudge anything."

"Thanks, Champa. I want to learn more about this stuff from you."

Champa grinned widely. "Absolutely. I'd love to help." She ran her fingers through my hair. "Now, let's work with your lovely curls."

Champa didn't do much with my hair. She just set my curls with some hair spray, commenting on how jealous she was of my curly hair.

"How do you know so much about makeup?" I asked.

Champa sighed. "When I was a tween, my classmates made fun of my dark complexion and called it ugly. That's why I started applying makeup and whitening products. However, with time, I learned to embrace my natural self. Now I do what feels good to me." She laughed. "There are days when I just scrunch my hair, stick a pencil through it, and go out in public. And others when I'm all dressed up. I like both sides of me. Whatever I do, I do it for me. Not to please others."

I hugged Champa again. "I'm sorry you had to go through that. You're absolutely gorgeous."

She smiled at me when we pulled away. "I know, and so are you. So, let's show everyone what you've got."

I sneaked a peek at myself one last time in the mirror and winked at my reflection. "Come on, beautiful. Let's break a leg."

***

I performed some of my favorite songs for the crowd, and they loved it. I was surprised when Grandpa Yu appeared on the stage out of nowhere and started singing a Cantonese song. He had a melodious voice, and the audience cheered for him. I played my guitar in such perfect sync with his voice that no one could tell we had never collaborated before.

"Let's hear it for Grandpa Yu. Woohoo!" I said to the audience, who were clapping, cheering, and whistling.

Grandpa Yu blushed, bowed, and thanked everyone before getting off the stage.

"My next song titled, 'Our Favorite Memories,' is about friendship," I announced. "This one's dedicated to the three people who taught me the real meaning of this word: Champa, Rory, and Desmond."

I sang the song I'd written for us.

"The four of us were strangers.

From different parts of the world.

Destiny brought us together.

When our lives overturned.

With no one else to rely on.

Other than each other.

We tried to move on.

By staying close together."

I raised my voice for the chorus.

"We laughed, we cried.

We sang, we enjoyed.

We told each other our stories.

We traveled, we explored.

We frolicked though we were broke.

It melted all our worries.

These will be our favorite memories."

I reduced the pace for the next stanza.

"Enjoying all our meals together.

Chatting and playing games all night.

Our silly jokes and our laughter.

All through the day and night.

Facing any obstacle that came our way.

Though it was dangerous.

We stuck together always.

It made us less nervous."

Again, I raised my voice for the chorus urging the crowd to sing along.

"We laughed, we cried.

We sang, we enjoyed.

We told each other our stories.

We traveled, we explored.

We frolicked though we were broke.

It melted all our worries.

These will be our favorite memories."

I got up from my seat and played the guitar, swinging it stylishly before the last part of the song.

"We've known each other only for ten days.

But we're closer than ever.

It feels like I've known them always.

And we'll be best friends forever.

Yes, yes, we'll be friends forever."

I signaled my audience to clap to the rhythm as I sang the chorus two more times before ending the song. Seeing Rory, Champa, and Desmond dance with the crowd made my heart burst with joy. Yuan's entire family, including the usually grumpy Grandpa Yu grooved to the music.

I turned the microphone toward my excited audience, urging them to sing the chorus lines one last time.

Suddenly, I felt as if my heart jumped into my mouth when I witnessed a man collapse on the floor. Though my eyes went wide with shock, I didn't stop playing the guitar. I composed myself and continued the performance as Yuan, his mother, and Grandpa Yu rushed to his side...it was Yuan's father. They quietly took him away, as discreetly as possible, as I sang the final line of the song slowly, trying not to let my voice shake.

"These will always be our favorite memories…"

Chapter 25

Rory

Champa, Desmond, and I helped Yuan carry his father outside the auditorium and laid him on a bench. Yuan loosened his father's shirt and performed CPR while Mrs. Yu called the emergency number. The rest of us took turns doing chest compressions until Yuan's uncle, a doctor, took over.

Soon, more of Yuan's relatives came and assured us they'd take care of the event in Yuan's family's absence. Less than fifteen minutes later, first responders arrived and took Yuan's father to the hospital. Yuan, his mother, and grandfather rode in the ambulance.

When we were about to go back to the auditorium, Champa exclaimed, "Des, you're bleeding."

Yuan's uncle, the doctor, looked at Desmond's hand. "You better get that checked at the ER. I'm driving to the hospital now to help my family. Why don't you come with me?"

"I'll come too," Champa said. She looked at Desmond. "Please don't refuse."

I gave Champa a page from my notebook with the public transport information. "Take this with you. It'll be helpful to find your way back."

"You can drive my car back when you've been seen by the doctor," the doctor said. "My wife is here. She'll take it home after the event."

"Thanks a lot for the offer, but we'll just take a bus or a cab back," Champa replied.

"Are you sure?" the doctor asked. "You're Yuan's friends, right? I saw you helping with the event this morning. I don't mind you driving my car."

"Are we allowed to drive here?" Desmond asked. "Champa and I are only seventeen."

"I'll come with you," I said. "I'm eligible to drive here."

Yuan's uncle dropped us at the hospital and gave us his car keys. We thanked him and requested him to ask his wife to inform Keira where we were. Champa took Desmond to the ER while I waited outside. The waiting area was crowded with no place to sit or stand. I decided to go back to the parking lot and wait for my friends.

But how would they know where I was?

Our "no cell phone" situation really sucked, and I was sick of it.

I went to a vending machine at the entrance to get a cup of coffee when I saw Grandpa Yu waiting in the line. He waved to me to stand next to him.

"You know, I've achieved a lot of things in life," Grandpa Yu started. "But I'm willing to trade all of it within a heartbeat in exchange for my son's life." He wept softly. "My only wish is for him to outlive me. I won't be able to take it if he leaves this world before me."

I placed my hand on his and held it lightly without saying anything. I listened quietly as he spoke about Mr. Yu's illness, and how it had shaken the Yu family.

Grandpa Yu had to leave when he got a call from Yuan. I offered to bring his coffee to him, and he gave me directions. After waiting in line for almost half an hour more, I got our drinks.

When I delivered Grandpa Yu his coffee, he told me Yuan's father was stable for now. He thanked our group for our help and wished us well.

I contemplated going back to the waiting room, but I didn't want to stand and drink my coffee. When I saw someone go into the emergency stairway, I followed them, hoping to sit and finish my drink.

As I let the hot beverage soothe my parched throat, I heard two familiar voices.

"How could my father do this to me, Champs?" Desmond wailed. "How could he make me believe that Ma abandoned us, when that wasn't true?"

"Maybe he wanted to protect you," Champa said quietly.

Desmond scoffed. "Protect me? By keeping me in the dark for so many years?" He sniffled. "You know how hard it was for me to find Ma. I searched for her for months." He pounded his fist on the wall. ""My father knew where she was all along, and they stayed in touch. I clearly heard him say to her, 'Love you, too, Han. See you in the evening' when I saw him earlier. Why did they keep this from me?"

"I understand how you feel, but please don't hurt yourself any further," Champa said. "You just got your wound treated and got a tetanus injection."

I felt bad for overhearing their conversation, but if I left now, they'd see me, since they were at the entrance.

"This pain is worse," Desmond replied, his voice breaking. "My parents didn't trust me, their son, to empathize with his mother's mental health situation. They thought I would reveal her secret to the entire world. Why else would they keep me in the dark?"

I felt a sharp pain in my chest as I remembered similar words from my mother. "Rory doesn't trust me, his mother, to tell me what's bothering him. Why else would he try to deal with his pain all alone?"

I had overheard my mother say this to my father on the camping trip last year, when I'd abruptly decided to return home after spending the whole trip glued to my cell phone screen. When I had come back to get something I'd forgotten, I had seen Mom crying to Dad.

I could feel a panic attack building inside as I recalled the horrible memory. One part of me wanted to hug my parents and tell them everything I was going through. But the more dominant part of me was in denial that I was affected by any of the unpleasant events of the past. So, I pretended I didn't hear anything and walked away.

Since that day, I hated myself more for upsetting my parents. I already felt like a failure for allowing myself to become a victim of a toxic relationship and for losing my real friends. But this incident made me *despise* myself.

I tried to calm down and took deep breaths as Champa spoke to Desmond in a soothing voice. "Your father is in the city. Are you going to meet with him?"

"Not today," Desmond answered.

"But you will in the future, right?"

Desmond laughed humorlessly. "If I keep my pain hidden and don't say anything, it will consume me completely."

Desmond was right. There was no point hiding my pain anymore.

Denying I wasn't okay was taking a toll on me.

Finally accepting it had made me feel better.

Talking about it with Keira and listening to her stories had made me feel less alone.

Now, I wanted to put the past behind me.

I didn't want to succumb to it anymore.

CHAPTER 26

Keira

After my performance, I was exhausted and hungry. I had eaten only a small veggie wrap and needed something more. I sat alone in the dressing room and munched on my emergency cookies, chips, and protein bar. I missed my friends and hoped they were alright. After eating, I decided to go back to the terrace.

On my way out, a lady introduced herself to me as Yuan's aunt and told me my friends were at the hospital to get someone's wound checked and would be back soon. I thanked her for the information.

I climbed up the stairs to the terrace slowly, wondering who was hurt and hoping they would be alright. But when I reached the top, I momentarily forgot about everything else.

The Victoria Peak Terrace had been my father's favorite place in Hong Kong. He spoke to me about it at least a dozen times every week. He loved the view from up here, but more than that, this was his special place, because he'd discovered something very important about himself.

"You'll know when you go there," he used to say with a mysterious look in his eyes. "It's my secret for now."

Whenever I sulked and pleaded with him to reveal details or at least give me a hint, he'd smile and promise that he'd bring me here himself one day. Though that day never came.

Being here today felt like it had, though.

Today was the day I'd finally learn my dear Pai's secret.

The one that changed his life.

There were thousands of locks with people's names along the walls of the Peak Terrace. Most were heart shaped with a couple's names engraved on them. There were also friendship bracelets, wall hangings, and other artifacts.

I sighed, doubting that I'd find my father's name among so many others.

Maybe I wasn't destined to learn his life-altering secret.

Not wanting to give up, I thought hard, trying to remember any clues he may have given me...

Eureka!

I found it.

There it was exactly like my father had described it: prominent only to those who searched for it—hidden otherwise.

When I spotted the rainbow-colored slinky spring toy, I ran my hand gingerly across the letters of his name: Miguel Delgado. With tears in my eyes, I recalled a memory I had forgotten until today.

"What's this?" I'd asked my father, looking at the metal spring-like thing in my hand.

"It's a slinky spring toy," my father said, his eyes twinkling. "See, it's got your names on it."

I stared at the weird metallic thing, not understanding why my father was so excited about it. Sure, it was colorful and had the letters of our names etched on it, but I really didn't get why this was our twelfth birthday present. What were we supposed to do with this?

"Come on, kids, it's a very special birthday present," my father said, hiding his disappointment. He had probably expected more enthusiasm from us.

"What's so special about it?" Sebastian asked.

Pai smiled. "It's got magical powers. You'll learn about it when the time comes."

"Really?" I asked. "You're not joking, right?"

Pai shook his head. "Really. I promise it's not a joke."

Now, I finally understood how those springy toys were magical.

Our father had given them to my brother and me to make us realize that we mattered the most to him.

And that I mattered the most to myself.

That I should love myself.

Accept myself.

And care about myself.

No matter what others said.

The spring was meaningful too.

My father had come here at a low point in his life. But that spring gave him the courage to bounce back and soar to heights he'd never imagined.

He wanted his children to soar too.

He wanted me to soar.

When my father left us, I had placed the slinky toy along with all his other memories inside a box and stowed it away safely in my closet.

I knew the first thing I had to do when I got back home.

I had to revive it.

And of course, myself.

Because that's what my dear Pai wanted.

And that's what I want.

CHAPTER 27

Rory

When Desmond and Champa left, I waited a few minutes before going downstairs and exiting the stairway on a different floor. I didn't want them to know I'd overheard their sensitive conversation. Though I felt guilty about it, I was grateful, because it had given me a new perspective about my life.

I went to the cafeteria to get us something to eat. I saw Desmond and Champa already waiting in the line, and I stood next to them. We bought some baked snacks, including a few vegetarian varieties for Keira. After eating, we drove back to Victoria Peak.

We parked the doctor's car, found his wife to return the keys, and headed toward the exit where the shuttle back home was waiting. Keira came running toward us, and seeing her smile made my heart skip a beat.

"I missed you guys," she said.

"Sorry, we couldn't tell you before we left to the hospital," Champa replied.

Keira shook her head. "No problem. Yuan's aunt informed me where you were." She turned to Desmond and pointed to his bandaged arm. "How's your hand?"

"I feel fine," Desmond answered. "So, I'm hungry again."

I laughed. "He's politely asking if you would share your snacks with him."

"What snacks?" Keira asked. "I finished my entire emergency stash."

"This one," Champa replied, giving Keira the paper bag with the baked goodies. When Desmond extended his hands toward the bag, she swatted them away playfully. "This is only for Keira."

"Thanks for the treats," Keira said. "But I can't finish all of this. I'm happy to share."

"Keira is my only real friend," Desmond declared, taking a savory cheesy veggie pastry from the bag.

"These are yum," Keira said, smacking her lips. "They're so fresh and melt in the mouth."

Champa patted her stomach. "Yes, we ate so much, I don't want dinner."

"It's just half past five," I reminded her. "You'll be hungry in less than an hour. I'd bet on it."

Champa stuck her tongue out at me. "I bet you'll be hungry before me."

We continued our banter until everyone else arrived, and we went inside the shuttle, going to the last row. Keira took the window seat, and I was about to sit next to her, when Champa took my place. I ended up sitting between her and Desmond.

When the shuttle started moving, Desmond and Champa fell asleep immediately. Seeing how Champa had been eager to sit next to Keira, I thought they'd chat the entire journey, but here she was, snoring softly.

When I was about to call her name, Keira tapped me on my shoulder. "I have something to show you."

"I want to see it," I replied. "But first I have something to say."

"Sure."

"I loved your surprise friendship song," I whispered. "You were simply awesome today." I handed her a permanent marker. "Can you sign my book, please? I've become your biggest fan."

Keira's eyes went wide. "You want my autograph?"

I nodded. "I'll flaunt it when you become famous."

Keira blushed. "Okay, thanks."

"Now I have something to show you," Keira said, taking a photograph from her pocket. "Miguel Delgado. That's my father's name. I found it on the Peak Terrace. Isn't that cool?"

I was touched that Keira shared something so personal with me. "That's amazing. I'm so glad for you." I looked at the picture closely. "Is that a slinky toy?"

She nodded. "Yes. My father also got one each for my brother and me with our names on them. I had forgotten about them until today."

"Are you going to hang yours next your father's the next time you're here?" I asked.

Keira shook her head. "I have only one. I want it close to me." She added quietly, "It was the last birthday present he ever gave me."

"I'm sorry, Keira. I shouldn't have said anything."

Keira shook her head. "Don't be sorry. You didn't say anything wrong. I'm happy to share this with someone who cares."

"Thanks."

"Instead, this is what I placed next to his name," Keira said, showing me another photo.

"A pink dolphin lock with all four of our names?"

Keira smiled. "Read what I wrote."

"'These will always be our favorite memories,'" I read aloud. "It's a line from your song."

Keira nodded. "Isn't it a perfect fit?"

"Indeed, it is," I agreed. "It's absolutely perfect."

Keira explained to me that this was her present for us. As Keira spoke, I couldn't help but feel sad about our trip coming to an end soon. In a few more days, we'd all be on our respective flights back home.

I knew the four of us would stay in touch, but what about Keira and me?

Would we continue our special relationship that didn't have a label?

Or was this just momentary?

Only time would tell.

***

We stopped for a moment at the store and picked up our suitcases, since it would be closed tonight. We walked back to our building and took the stairs because the elevator was full. The four of us dragged our suitcases and walked to our apartment as Keira talked about her present for us. I pretended I was hearing about it for the first time, as decided with Keira earlier.

"You're the best, Keira Delgado," Champa said, hugging Keira.

"This is the best present ever," Desmond added, clutching his copy of the photo tightly. "Thank you for taking enough pictures for all of us.

"Hey, are my eyes playing tricks, or is the lock broken again?" Champa asked suddenly, rubbing her eyes.

We sighed in unison. "Not this again."

A woman in uniform showed us her police badge. "Are you staying in this apartment?"

Her colleague held up our group photo in his hands to confirm we were the same people in the picture. "Tell us the truth."

Keira stepped forward. "Yes, we are temporarily staying here until we go back to our respective countries."

"Officer, did they get scammed like us too?" a guy around our age asked.

"Sir, let *us* handle this, please." The officer turned to us. "Why were you staying here instead of a hotel?"

"We had nowhere else to go," I answered. "Mr. and Mrs. Hong left us here after taking our money."

"The same thing happened to us," one of the teens from the other group said. "The Hongs picked us up from the airport and dumped us here!"

"Why didn't you file a police report?" the officer asked me.

"We didn't want to be asked to leave," Desmond replied.

"We need all eight of you to come to the police station," the officer said. "We have more questions."

We followed the two officers to the police station, where they questioned us individually. I was relieved they didn't treat us like criminals, but they noted our personal information, including our movements about the city and what we had done when we were in Hong Kong. After the questioning, they asked us to wait in a large room together.

While waiting, the eight of us exchanged stories. The other group was intrigued by our adventures in Hong Kong without our phones.

"I can't believe you guys actually survived without your devices for so long," Ben from the other group said. "I brought my phone with me. I had hidden it in my bag."

Afia, his friend laughed. "Ben's purpose of coming to the Mobile Rehab was to vlog about it. He's been uploading videos on social media since the beginning of this trip."

"Show them the latest video we took before we called the police," Amar, Afia's brother said. "It's already got over a thousand views."

"Actually, it has thirty thousand views now," Becca, the other girl in their group said, showing her friends the phone. "Most of the comments confirm Desmond's identity as an actor. The online search engines were right."

The video showed the photo of the four of us: the one we had placed on the windowsill in our apartment. It went on to talk about us using the information from our social media accounts, focusing on Desmond's fame as a former actor.

"Did you upload our photo on social media?" Desmond asked. "How could you do that without our permission?"

"Just chill, dude," Ben said. "It's not a big deal. You should be happy you're getting publicity because of us."

"Please delete it," Keira requested. "We don't want to be a part of your vlog."

Before anyone from their group could respond, one of the police officers returned. "You're all free to go. We'll investigate the Hongs." He turned toward Desmond. "Sir, please come with me."

"Can my friends come too?" Desmond asked.

"Yes, that's not a problem."

Before we followed the officer out of the room, Champa glared at the other group about to leave. "We'd really appreciate it if you deleted our video."

The four just exited the room without another word.

I didn't think they would comply with our request.

And we couldn't really do anything about it.

Chapter 28

Keira

Desmond's eyes looked like they would fall out of their sockets. "W—What are *you* doing here?"

"We called your father," the officer answered.

"I'm glad they did," Desmond's father said. "Because I didn't know where to look for you when you disappeared earlier."

"Did you contact my mother too?" Keira asked the police officer.

"What about my parents?" Champa added.

"I said I would take responsibility for all four of you for now," Mr. Tan replied. "But you have a lot to explain."

Desmond's father asked us to wait in his car while he spoke to the police in private. The driver opened the door, and we got inside the massive seven-seater vehicle.

"I can't believe you lied to your mother and me," Mr. Tan said sitting next to his son. "Why did you have to do that?"

"Look who's talking," Desmond mumbled audibly.

"Champa, I didn't expect this from you," Mr. Tan continued. "I thought you were sensible."

Champa didn't say anything.

"And Rory Matthews and Keira Delgado, was it? The police told me you're both nineteen. You're *adults*. At least you both should've driven some sense into these two." Mr. Tan shook his head. "The police told me you got conned because of some social media video. What were you all thinking?"

None of us dared to utter a single word.

Mr. Tan took a deep breath. "Anyway, what's done is done. From now on, I'm in charge of you kids, and here's what's going to happen. You'll stay with us tonight in Desmond's grandparents' house, contact your families, and take the earliest flight back to your respective countries. I'll pay for your journeys. Is that clear?"

"Thanks, Mr. Tan, that's very generous of you," I said. "But I can't accept your money. I can manage for a couple more days…"

"Keira, I *insist*. If you don't accept my decision, the police will contact your parents. And I know you don't want that."

"Then please let me pay you back when I get home, sir," I requested.

"I'll wire you the money, too, Mr. Tan," Rory added.

"Fine," Desmond's father agreed. He placed his hand on his son's arm. "*We* have a lot to discuss."

***

"Let's give Desmond and Champa some space to talk to Desmond's family," Rory whispered to me when the driver entered the building where Desmond's grandparents lived. "How about you and I go for a walk in the meantime?"

I nodded. "I like that idea."

Champa chimed in. "Desmond's grandparents will be very upset if you eat outside."

"Champa is right." Mr. Tan gave us a piece of paper with the full address. "We'll be expecting you for dinner."

"We'll be back in thirty minutes," I promised.

I thought about the goodbye present I had for Rory in my pocket. Would he get too overwhelmed if I gave it to him now? Would he feel too seen? After all, we'd shared our most personal feelings with each other because we felt safe that our paths would never cross again, right? Would it be best to never talk to each other again?

"Once we get back, I'm going to create a text group for the four of us," Champa said, interrupting my anxious thoughts. "What should we name it?"

"My Boos," Desmond answered right away, referring to our silly t-shirts, obviously forgetting his father was still in the car. He hadn't said anything during the ride, but he seemed to be a little more at ease now.

Champa giggled. "Perfect."

"Are you serious?" Rory asked. "Come on, we can find something else."

"Nope." Champa shook her head vehemently. "My Boos is perfect."

"And the profile picture that can never ever be changed will be our iconic group photograph," Desmond declared.

I smiled, remembering the silly photo we had taken in our hilarious "couple pajama sets" with ghosts on them.

Mr. Tan chuckled, but he didn't ask us any questions.

I laughed. "I like the idea."

"When you can't beat them, join them," Rory stated with a sigh. "I'm in too."

"Great," Desmond said. "And we're here."

I got out of the car. "Rory and I will see you all in a bit."

"Leave your luggage here," Mr. Tan said. "We'll take them."

Rory and I walked slowly to the convenience store at the end of the street in comfortable silence. We bought a box of assorted exotic fruits for Desmond's family. It was expensive, but we still got it, since we were having a meal at their place on such short notice.

We got two small cups of coffee at the vending machine to access the store seating area. There was a sign board that read, "Please leave after you finish your meal or beverage, and let other customers sit. Thank you."

Rory chuckled and pointed at it as we sat at the only vacant table. "That's a nice way to ask people to buzz off."

I laughed. "That refers particularly to people like us, who get beverages just to sit here."

Rory nodded. "I won't take much time then." He opened his bag and placed a book on the table. "I wanted to give you this."

"The signed copy of Walt Lauren's latest book," I whisper-squealed, delighted. "Are you sure you want to give this to me? It's addressed to you."

"Come to Strollfield to return this to me and get your own copy from Walt," Rory said. He took a long sip of his coffee. "Can you open it?" Rory's face had a pink tinge to it, and he avoided meeting my eyes.

I opened the book and immediately knew why.

Inside was a neatly folded sheet of paper.

I looked at it and gasped. "This is beautiful," I exclaimed. "Is that me?"

Rory nodded shyly.

I couldn't tear my eyes off the drawing. I looked gorgeous sitting on the stairs at the Big Buddha. I had a serene smile on my face that Rory had sketched perfectly. It was the moment when I was fondly remembering my father.

"I'm speechless, Rory," I said, still not looking away from the paper. "Thank you so much for the gift. I simply love it."

Rory laughed nervously. "I'm relieved. I'm an amateur and didn't know if it was good enough." He added after another sip of his coffee, "This is a return gift for the present you gave me. You captured me on camera at the perfect moment at the beach last week."

I smiled. "That was nothing compared to this."

"It was not nothing," Rory said, raising his voice a little bit. The pink color on his cheeks deepened. "It means a lot to me."

"Thanks." I placed the paper back inside the novel. "This is one of the best presents I've ever received."

"The novel or the drawing?"

I felt my cheeks go warm. "The drawing."

We drank our beverages quietly. I had so much more to say, but I didn't. My hands fiddled with the envelope meant for Rory in my jeans pocket. Maybe I could give it to him some other time.

Rory had not used the words, "goodbye present." I was going to take that as a cue that he, too, wanted us to meet again in the future.

Until then, I would cherish our wonderful memories together.

We walked back to Desmond's grandparents' house in complete silence. I realized this was probably the last time we'd be alone on this trip.

We had held hands easily these days, but today that seemed tough. I was scared I wouldn't be able to let go.

"Rory—" I said, at the same time he said *my* name.

Rory laughed. "You go first."

"Thank you for convincing me to sign up for the Mobile Rehab at the airport that day. If you had not done that, I would have never gotten to meet you and our wonderful friends."

Rory smiled and squeezed my hand.

We walked to the building elevator. I wanted to hug him, but I was scared the tears that I was trying so hard to hold in would flow out in a flash.

I felt a little better when I noticed Rory wipe his eyes against his shirt sleeve.

It was reassuring that both of us didn't want to say goodbye.

CHAPTER 29

Rory

I wanted to tell Keira I was glad I met her and that I had a wonderful time with her during the trip, but I was afraid my voice would break. I was embarrassed for feeling this way. It was unlike me to get emotional. After all, I was excellent at hiding how I felt.

But in the last ten days, I had shared a part of myself with Keira that I hadn't shown anyone else. Initially, it was because she was a stranger I'd never see again. But soon, I found myself thinking it wouldn't be such a bad thing if we continued talking.

I wasn't sure if the tears in my eyes were because I would miss Keira. Or because I was afraid of feeling lonely again with no one to talk to.

I wished I was back to when I could hold it all inside. I didn't want to deal with these overwhelming feelings. It was annoying. I couldn't even ask Keira for a hug because of my stupid emotions. What if I burst into tears and made a fool of myself?

Out of the corner of my eye, I saw Keira blinking back her own tears.

Was she crying because she'd miss me too?

Somehow that made me feel better.

"Why is the elevator taking so long?" Keira asked.

I was surprised that Keira's voice sounded completely normal. Didn't she have tears in her eyes just a few seconds ago?

I cleared my throat to prevent my own voice from breaking. "It must be a pain for the apartment residents."

"Rory, we are standing near the service elevator," Keira pointed to the sign, laughing. "This is the wrong one."

I shook my head and laughed with her. "I'm too hungry to think straight."

That was a lie. I was too "in my head."

"Same here," Keira replied. "Let's head to the residential elevators."

We finally reached Desmond's grandparents' apartment with the sign board "The Li Family" and knocked on the door.

A friendly elderly man opened the door. "Oh, there you are. I was going to come to get you myself."

"Sorry," I said, sheepishly. "We waited near the service elevator without realizing our mistake."

The man, who introduced himself as Desmond's grandfather, Mr. Li, laughed loudly. "I'm not surprised. That happens to almost everyone who comes here for the first time."

Keira and I laughed with him politely before following him inside.

Though the living room was not that big, it was luxurious. The living room had an expensive leather sofa set and a television table surrounded by a vintage bookshelf, which doubled as a showcase for exclusive collectibles.

Desmond's grandfather sat down on an antique rocking chair made of teak. It had exquisite carvings that made it look even more classy. "Why don't you both take a seat? Dinner will be ready shortly."

Keira bowed. "Sorry, I was too busy admiring your lovely home that I forgot my manners. I'm Keira Delgado. Thank you for having us, today."

"And my name is Rory Matthews," I added, bowing with Keira. I used both my hands to give the fruit box to Desmond's grandfather, like I had read about in a cultural etiquette magazine. "This is a small token of gratitude from both of us."

"My, my, what wonderful friends my grandson has." Desmond's grandfather beamed at us. "It's our pleasure to host you today."

"So, that's why both of you disappeared." An older woman entered, taking the fruits from her husband. She smiled at us. "You shouldn't have taken so much effort."

Keira and I introduced ourselves and greeted the woman who said she was Desmond's grandmother, Mrs. Li. She led us to the dining area, which had a large table that was already set with porcelain plates and silver cutlery. Two people wearing aprons filled the empty spaces with bowls of piping hot food.

"Desmond told me you don't eat meat, Keira. We have a separate spread for you."

Keira's eyes went wide at the variety of dishes placed on the table. "Thank you so much."

"It's no problem," Desmond's grandmother said. "Take a seat. Champa is talking to her parents and Desmond's with his. Everyone will be out shortly."

From the dining area, the apartment looked massive. There was a large kitchen, and a passage that led to the bedrooms and a bathroom. On one side of the passage, there was a glass shelf with what looked like priceless artifacts. And there were beautiful paintings and photographs displayed on the wall. Champa wasn't joking when she said Desmond's family was wealthy.

Keira and I waited for everyone else at the table. Being the only ones here was a little awkward, but I was not complaining. I got to ogle the amazing-looking traditional Cantonese dishes. There were three types of dumplings: steamed, pan-fried, and deep-fried; a variety of dishes with colorful vegetables and tender pieces of meat or seafood in luscious gravies; noodles and rice.

The vegetarian offerings had the same dishes but in smaller portion sizes.

Desmond and Champa entered with wide grins on their faces, followed by Desmond's parents.

Keira and I stood up to shake hands with them and were introduced to Mrs. Tan. Desmond's grandparents arrived soon after, and we began eating.

For the first few minutes, no one spoke. Everyone concentrated on their food, which was delicious. I was expecting the dishes to taste the same as the ones we had eaten at restaurants. But these were more flavorful.

Desmond's father, Mr. Tan, finally broke the silence. "So, how was ten days without mobile phones?"

Desmond groaned. "Terrible."

At the same time, the other three of us said, "It wasn't that bad."

Mr. Li laughed and turned toward his grandson. "Why was it so terrible?"

"It was tough," Desmond answered. "We couldn't look up important stuff online. We couldn't call anyone when we needed to. And I missed texting so much."

Desmond went on to explain more about the non-working phone, as everyone laughed. We also shared all our other mishaps.

"But we learned conversations are way better than phones during meals," I said. "And card games with friends are way more fun than short videos."

Desmond's grandmother clasped her hands together. "That's why our generation had more fun than you youngsters."

"We learned that knowing how to read a paper map is very handy," Keira added. "And that it's good to remember some emergency phone numbers instead of depending on your phone."

"Sounds like you got some basic life skills," Mr. Li teased.

Champa laughed. "We sure did. And now all of us can *do our business* without having a smartphone in our hands."

The table was filled with roars of laughter.

"I'm sorry we weren't more helpful," Desmond's mother said when our laughter died down. "We had no idea Desmond and Champa were having troubles in their school."

"Thank you for taking care of our children," Desmond's father added.

"We all took care of each other," Keira replied. "We almost forgot Desmond and Champa were younger than us. They are ace problem-solvers."

"That's excellent," Desmond's grandmother said. "Let's hear the takeaways and lessons learned from our two high school students here."

"I'll carry my mobile phone with me whenever I travel in the future, but I will not depend on it. Maps, flashlights, a notebook with important contact numbers, and lots of spare food and water will be a must in my bag," Desmond said.

Champa nodded. "I'll do everything Des said. Plus, I'll change my digital habits on a daily basis as well. I plan to limit my time spent on games and short videos during my free time. Instead, I'll focus on building stuff with my hands. I genuinely enjoy that. And, of course, I'll devote more time to learning about insects." She paused for a moment. "Just because others think my interests are boring doesn't mean I should stop."

"Way to go," Desmond's mother said. "Do what *you* love, always. Don't let others define what's fun for you. I learned that the hard way too."

"Rory and Keira, do you have anything to add?" Mr. Tan asked.

"I'd like to use my phone to stay in touch with the people I care about," Keira replied. "Sometimes, just asking someone how they are makes a big difference."

"That's a great point," Mrs. Li said. "That's the only thing I use my phone for." She turned to me. "How about you, Rory?"

I hesitated a little. "Um, I want to stop treating my phone as my companion. It's just a device."

Mr. Tan agreed. "We all need to stop doing that. Getting lost in that small screen is so easy that we think it's a part of us."

Desmond's mother clapped her hands. "Well, kudos to the four of you for making your nondigital trip worthwhile. Let's have dessert to celebrate."

We ate a variety of tarts, puddings, and pies for dessert while chatting. Desmond's family made me laugh so many times during our meal. I could see where he got his amazing sense of humor from.

After dinner, I was so full, I couldn't get up from my chair. But I forced myself to stand. I had to reschedule my flight and contact my family.

***

Later, when I opened my email using Desmond's grandparents' computer in their study, I was delighted to see an email from Tina.

I read her email out loud. "Hey, R, are you alright? Jai showed me a video of you on social media. It said you and many others were conned out of your money. We hope you're safe. We're worried about you. Reply when you see this. Love, T."

"I'm so jealous," Keira said from behind me. "You have friends worrying about you."

"How did someone in Canada watch that video?" Desmond asked. "It's not even viral."

I didn't really care if we were trending on social media or not. I was elated that my friends cared to find out if I was okay. I replied to Tina's email, informing her I was alright.

I rescheduled my flight and composed an email to my parents, letting them know I would be arriving the next day.

"Guys, can we do a group hug?" Champa asked as I was about to get up from my chair and let Keira take my place.

"Of course," Desmond replied, ushering me closer.

Keira hugged Champa first. Desmond and I embraced them.

We held each other for a long time, not wanting to let go.

CHAPTER 30

Keira

On the one hand, I wished we'd stay in this group hug forever, but on the other, I wanted to pull away. The separation anxiety was setting in, and I was scared I'd burst into uncontrollable tears. Champa and Desmond were already crying, threatening to start my waterworks, but I managed to hold them back. Because my tears would not be out of love for these people but resentment.

Champa and Desmond had each other, Rory had caring friends, but I would be all alone. And these three would probably forget me. If I started crying now, I would feel guilty for my pessimistic thoughts.

We pulled away when we heard a knock on the door. It was Desmond's mother, who came to inform Champa that her mother had called again. Champa left with Mrs. Tan. Rory and Desmond followed soon after.

I was relieved to be alone while checking my email. It would have been embarrassing if the other three had seen my empty inbox. Tears welled up in my eyes again, but I wiped them away. I had to stop this self-pity and start embracing myself. That's what my father would have wanted for me.

I rubbed my palms together and hit the compose button to send myself an email.

Dearest Pai,

I promise to love and care for myself like you want me to.

Just continue to watch over me.

Love,

Keira

My heart felt lighter when I hit the send button.

I then opened the airline website to reschedule my flight. There was only one flight for tomorrow, and it was going to depart in four hours. I had to be at the airport in an hour if I wanted to make it on time.

I went to the guest room and brought my bags to the living room where everyone was sitting.

"Keira, where are you off to so soon?" Champa asked.

"My flight is in four hours," I said. "It's the only one departing tomorrow."

"I'll drop you at the airport," Desmond's grandfather offered, getting up from the couch.

"We'll come along," Desmond said as Champa and Rory also got up.

We waited near the building entrance while Mr. Li went to get the car from the parking lot. Champa and Desmond voiced their disappointment about me leaving earlier than planned. They said that they were planning to play games all night tonight. Rory was quiet.

When Mr. Li brought the car, Desmond got into the front seat. Champa, Rory, and I climbed at the back, with Rory sitting between Champa and me. I offered Rory my seat, knowing how uncomfortable the middle seat would be for him, but he didn't let me switch.

"It's a short distance," Rory whispered. "It's easier to get out of the car from a door seat. Besides, I don't want to miss this."

He held out his hand casually. I took it and intertwined our fingers, enjoying the warmth of his touch throughout the ride.

When we reached the airport, I only had time to get out and take my suitcase from the trunk. The traffic police were monitoring vehicle arrivals because of the crowd. They didn't even let me stand there and wave goodbye to my friends. I was glad I'd bid farewell to them properly earlier.

Though the airport was crowded, I got through the check-in and security check processes quickly. I sat near the departure gate with more than two hours to kill. My mind was whirling with thoughts about everyone back home. It was almost time to face reality.

I planned how to break up with Diego. It would be best to do it in person, though he didn't deserve my time. But I was not the type of person to end things over a text.

Diego had never been good for me. I saw it many times, but I continued our relationship because he had been a part of my life for a long time. Him being my brother's best friend, bandmate, and my mother's favorite didn't help either.

But things with Diego weren't always bad. When we started dating, we were inseparable. We made excuses to spend time together in high school. We even sneaked out of our class a few times just to hang out.

However, he was toxic when either of us were feeling down. He hid his emotions and disliked it when I tried to care for him. And when I was upset, he demeaned me. We weren't emotionally available for each other. I felt lonely many times when I was with him.

But then, I felt lonely with *everyone* back home—my mother, Sebastian, *and* my friends. I felt like I didn't matter when I was around them. I thought it was normal and didn't bother much about it.

After all, other than my father, no one really liked me for me—the sensitive Keira Delgado, who felt intense emotions and loved deep conversations. So I tried to change myself. And lost a sense of who I really was.

Now, after connecting with my father again through his experiences, I want to find myself again.

My original authentic self.

I was going to be me, at least when I was by myself. I wanted to translate my passionate emotions into my music and songs, even if it was offbeat. I would try to surround myself with people who enjoyed my company. And most importantly, I would stay away from those who made me feel terrible about myself.

I knew it wouldn't be easy. It would mean letting go of the people in my life right now and making new friends.

The past ten days had taught me that it was worth letting new people into my life. They might not be with me in the future, but they had left a deep impact on my mind.

And that was enough for now to keep me going.

***

I was like a zombie during the flight back home, sleeping throughout. I only woke up for bathroom and meal breaks, and when there was a layover in between. When we reached Brazil, I was wide awake, ready for the next chapter of my life.

When I entered our house, I was glad no one was around. Sebastian was still holidaying with Diego, Marina, and Savio. And my mother was at work.

I went to my room, opened my closet, and reached for the cardboard box that I had placed behind my clothes and other belongings. It was my secret treasure that no one was allowed to touch.

I opened the box and went through every item inside it. They were all memories of my father that I cherished the most. It had my cards and letters to him, gifts he'd given me, and lots of photographs of us. I spent a long time remembering him fondly while talking to him softly.

When I found the slinky toy with my name on it, I took it out carefully and wiped it off. I placed it in my backpack, put everything else back in its place, and headed back to my dormitory.

In my dorm room, I hung the slinky where I could see it every day from my desk. It was a reminder that my father had given me the best present ever—me.

I was not ugly or boring. Neither did I need to be fixed, nor did I have to change myself.

I was fine as I was.

I was me.

I admired the new addition to my room for a few minutes before getting my books ready for my classes next week. After completing my work, I opened my drawer, switched on my phone, and charged it.

I went through the notifications on my device. As expected, I didn't have too many. Sebastian had sent me an "okay" as a reply to the text I'd sent him before leaving for Hong Kong ten days ago:

> **Me:** I'm not coming on the trip with you and our friends. I'm going somewhere else for ten days. Don't try to contact me. I'm leaving my phone here. Inform our mother.

> **Sebastian:** Okay

If I had read my brother's monosyllable response ten days ago, I would have been furious, but now, I found it amusing. He didn't care about me as much as I did about him.

None of them did.

There was not a single text or voicemail from my mother, brother, or so-called friends.

Well, this would make it easier for me to let go of them. I didn't plan on cutting ties with them completely, but I would not give them as much importance in my life.

I laughed humorlessly when I read the only other notification on my phone. It was an instant message from a plastic surgery clinic.

I called my mother immediately.

"Hello, Mother," I said in an even tone when she picked up. It took every milligram of my willpower not to shout at her. "How are you doing?"

"Keira? Are you back from your trip or whatever?"

"Yes, I'm back." I took a deep breath. "What's this notification about an appointment next week? Why did you book it without talking to me?"

"I thought you wanted it," my mother replied.

"No, Mother, I don't," I said slowly, emphasizing every word. "I do not need or want any 'fixing up' whatsoever."

My mother sighed. "Are you sure? It can help you get back with Diego, you know."

"I am *not* getting back together with Diego," I emphasized. "*Ever.*"

"But plastic surgery helped me, Keira."

"I know it did," I said. "And I'm happy for you. I'm not against plastic surgery or anyone getting it. But I don't want it, and I want you to respect my choice."

"Alright, suit yourself." She paused for a moment. "Come over for dinner tomorrow. Your brother will be back from his trip."

"Okay, I will."

"See you then."

"Um, Mother, aren't you going to ask me where I went?"

"If I ask, will you tell me?"

"I went to Hong Kong," I answered. "To the same place as Pai."

"Cool."

There was another awkward pause.

"Okay, Keira. See you tomorrow."

Surprisingly, I was okay after talking to my mother. I was kind of glad she wanted me to come over. It was her way of making up with me. I decided to accept it.

I put my phone aside and opened the novel by Walt Lauren that Rory had gifted me.

I smiled at the thought of him sitting next to me during the ride to the airport just to hold my hand, despite being uncomfortable in the middle seat.

Rory Matthews.

I wondered if he had reached home safely. I picked up my phone, saved his number, and texted him.

> **Me:** Hey, I hope you reached home safely. Send me the videos from our trip when you get a chance.

CHAPTER 31

Rory

Desmond, Champa, and I were on the same flight for most of our journey back home. We sat together in the aircraft and couldn't stop talking about Keira the whole time.

"I miss her so much," Champa said. "It's so unfair she lives in a different country. I wonder if she got back safely."

"I'll create our messaging group as soon as we get back," Desmond replied. "We can stay in touch often then."

"Why did she have to leave suddenly last night?" Champa complained. "It would have been so nice if we could have spent more time together."

I wished Champa would stop talking about Keira. It made me think about her as well. But I didn't want to do that. I couldn't let my feelings for her grow any more than they already had.

It was nice when we spent time together and poured our hearts out. Now it was time to face the reality that she was many miles away and go about my life. After all, out of sight was out of mind, right?

I fell asleep on my aisle seat while listening to the other two reminisce about our wonderful trip. It was hard to believe that the three of us preferred to converse or sleep, rather than switch on our inflight entertainment systems. This would have been impossible for us ten days ago.

When we reached our layover airport, Desmond and Champa proceeded to their connecting aircraft, and I headed to mine. We said bye to each other comfortably, since our cities were just a two-hour flight from each other. It would be easy for us to meet if we wanted to.

I had a harder time without my phone on my second flight since I was alone. This aircraft didn't have inflight entertainment, so everyone was engrossed in their cell phones. I distracted myself by doodling in my notebook. I had a lot of things to think about, but decided to put that off until I got home.

When I reached Strollfield, I was surprised to see my mother pick me up at the airport, as it was during her work hours.

"Mom!" I yelled and ran to her, hugging her tightly.

She laughed. "How did you like my surprise?"

"I love it," I answered, touched that she drove over two hours just to pick me up. "Did you cancel your appointments for me?"

"I wanted to ensure you were alright. I was worried after watching the videos on social media."

"I'm fine," I replied. "I had a great time."

"Good. How about we have lunch together before heading to your place?"

"I would love that," I said, linking arms with her. "Let's go."

On the way, I told my mother everything about our trip. She listened to me intently, asking questions in between. She couldn't stop laughing when I mentioned her eldest child's prank on me.

"Can you believe Riley made me groove to her voice?" I said, failing to keep a straight face. "And she was talking about the human digestive system."

"Your sister is hilarious."

I nodded, still laughing. "It's funny now. But back then, I was wondering what hit me."

My mother pulled over at the parking lot of our favorite poutine restaurant. This was the place my parents always brought me to when they wanted to have a heart-to-heart talk with me. The last time we came here was when I told them I wanted to change my major a few months ago.

We sat at a booth and looked at the menu, though we knew it really well. My mother received a text from someone.

"Is that Dad?" I asked.

My mother nodded. "He has an emergency and can't make it." She set her phone aside. "It's just the two of us then."

We ordered our food and talked while waiting.

"I'm sorry we didn't check the Mobile Rehab more carefully," my mother said.

I shook my head. "No, Mom. We went through their brochure thoroughly. They are really good at conning people."

"It's a relief that you're okay. Your father, Riley, and I weren't able to sleep last night." She took a sip of her water. "Tina and Jai were with us the whole time too."

"How did you find out?" I asked. "Did Tina and Jai tell you?"

"Riley told us. She called Tina immediately, who came over with Jai right away."

"Whoa," I exclaimed. "Tina and Jai drove all the way at night?"

My mother nodded. "We were also surprised to see them."

I grinned widely. "I'm glad so many people care about me."

My mother's expression turned serious. "Of course we do." She hesitated before continuing. "I would have never let you go on this trip. But your screen addiction was getting out of hand. So I hoped the rehab would help you."

"I get panic attacks, Mom," I admitted without meeting her eyes. "I haven't been okay."

My mother opened her mouth to speak but stopped midway, because the server brought our food. I couldn't bear to see the anxious look on Mom's face.

"Rory, why didn't you tell us about it?" Mom asked when the server had left.

I looked down. "I was embarrassed." I ate a fry from my poutine. "I thought ignoring it or diverting my mind would help. But it made everything worse." I sighed. "I know I can't escape it now, so I've decided to get professional help. I want to try therapy."

"Why were you embarrassed? Your father and I would have understood."

"I thought my issues were too trivial," I replied. "And that I was weak."

"We wouldn't have judged you."

I raised my voice a little. "I know, Mom." I evened my tone again. "You, Dad, and Riley are great. I never doubted any of you. It was *me*. *I* didn't want to face it."

"I'm proud of you. Therapy is a good idea. And remember, we're here for you."

I smiled. "Thanks. I'm sorry for being on my phone and walking out abruptly during our last camping trip. I shouldn't have done that."

She patted the back of my hand. "It's okay. You can make it up to us by planning our next one."

"Deal."

My mother dropped me in Strollfield—where my university was—and headed back to my hometown, Duckville. When I entered my apartment, my friends, Jai and Tina, came running from our living room couch.

"Oh, thank goodness you're back safely," Tina yelled, hugging me.

Jai gave me a friendly thump on my back. "It's great to see you, roommate."

"I'm fine, guys," I said, secretly pleased to see my friends fussing over me. Before I went on the trip, it felt like they didn't include me in their plans. "Stop worrying now."

"Okay then, go freshen up," Tina replied. "Afterwards, let's catch up."

I took a long warm shower, got dressed, and switched on my phone. It felt strange to hold the device in my hands after so many days. Instinctively, my fingers navigated to the social media app and scrolled to the short videos. I had still not overcome this habit.

However, unlike before, I realized immediately that I didn't mean to do that. Instead, I opened my text messaging app. I had messages from Dad and Riley asking me if I was well. I replied to them.

When I scrolled through the other notifications, one of them made me smile. I guessed who sent it to me, even if I didn't have her number saved in my phone.

I added the number to my contacts. Keira Delgado.

> **Keira:** Hey, I hope you reached home safely. Send me the videos from our trip when you get a chance.

> **Me:** Hey, I'm safely at home. How about you? How was your journey? I'll send you the videos soon.

"Rory, do you need more time?" Jai asked from the living room.

"Put your phone away and come here," Tina said. "Let's hang out."

I placed my phone on the charger and went to the living room.

"You didn't bring your phone with you?" Tina teased. "The rehab seems to have worked."

"It has definitely *started* to work," I replied. "I have a long way to go though."

"Give us some tips to stay away from our devices," Jai said.

"I'm good," Tina said. "I'm not glued to my phone all the time."

Jai scoffed. "Oh please. You're chatting with your boyfriend all the time."

"Hey, that doesn't count," Tina protested.

"It does," Jai replied. "So does e-reading novels."

"Reading is a great habit. How is that phone addiction? Then what about your online chess games?"

"Chess stimulates the brain," Jai countered.

As Jai and Tina went on arguing, I realized something. All of us were attached to our smartphones. There were so many things we could do with them: stay in touch with friends we couldn't meet every day, look up any information we needed within minutes, read any book from any part of the world, complete tasks in a short time, and get unlimited hours of entertainment. Our cell phones were amazing.

However, life outside the digital world wasn't bad either. It was fun talking to friends and playing games. And there was immense joy in getting lost in our planet's natural beauty: colorful rainbows, lush greenery, picturesque sunsets, and pristine beaches. Besides, there were so many things to do without our devices—play sports, build stuff, compose songs, and pursue so many other interests.

The key was to get the best of both worlds.

And Mobile Rehab had taught me to do just that.

Epilogue

A few days later on a Friday night

My Boos

Champa: Has everyone shared all the photos and videos from our trip?

Desmond: Yes

Rory: Yeah

Keira: Yup. I scanned and sent you everything I have.

Desmond: Keira, the pic of you and Rory is missing. I'm referring to the one with the couple clothes.

Champa: The one we took on the same day we clicked our profile picture.

Keira: I lost that one.

Rory: Can't we change our profile photograph? Please? We have so many better ones. How about one of the dolphin keychain Keira gave us?

Desmond: Nope. We can't change our display pic.

Desmond: @Rory: I've framed Keira's present. So has Champa. We can't scan it now.

Champa: Never. Our photo is perfect as is.

Champa: @Rory: I love Keira's dolphin keychain, but a profile pic must have our faces.

Desmond: @Keira: That's sad. That was a great picture.

Desmond: @everyone: I've got to run. I'm trying to make my own sunscreen. I love the one in the AMZ kit and want to try and replicate it.

Rory: @Desmond: That's fantastic. Send me a sample when you're done.

Rory: @everyone: I'm starting open-water swimming tomorrow. Wish me luck!

Champa: @Rory: Good luck. Have fun.

Champa: @everyone: I'm going to study. Trying again for the biology Olympiad this year. I'm so nervous.

Keira: @Champa: You'll kill it. Don't worry.

Keira: @everyone: I'm going to sleep. It's past midnight here.

Private Chats On The Same Night

Rory and Desmond

Desmond: I need your help with a math sum.

Rory: My high school math is rusty. Why don't you ask Champa?

Desmond: Champa is great at a lot of things. Teaching is not one of them.

Rory: LOL. Okay, I'll give it a try. I'll call you tomorrow. I'm off to play chess with my roommate now.

Desmond: Your doctor roommate? Do you have a chance of winning at all?

Rory: I don't. But it's okay. I win at every-thing else.

Desmond: LOL. Have fun.

Keira and Champa

Keira: I gave Marina a piece of my mind today. She commented on my appearance again.

Champa: I'm so happy for you. What did you say? Give me all the details.

Keira: I told her no matter how much make-up she uses, she won't be able to conceal the ugliness inside her.

Champa: ROFL. I can't stop laughing. She deserves it.

Keira: Don't get me wrong. I'm not against makeup. But Marina was getting on my nerves.

Champa: I got what you meant. You don't need to justify. Sending you a big hug.

Keira: Thank you. Sending you a tight hug too. By the way, I painted my toenails. Check this pic.

Champa: Love it. The color is amazing. It suits you.

Keira: All thanks to you. Your suggestion was great.

Champa: Aww. You're so sweet. I really wish you were here.

Keira: Did your classmates give you a hard time again?

Champa: Not really. They've maintained a low profile since Desmond's and my parents had a talk with our teachers.

Keira: I'm glad things are better with you, but your classmates deserve to be punished. If they trouble you again, vent to me. We'll send them bad karma together.

Champa: I'd love that. Thank you. Hey, sorry for keeping you awake.

Keira: I'm not going to sleep. I said so because I want to read my novel without any disturbance.

Champa: LOL. Okay, I'll get back to studying.

Keira: Just so you know, you can message me at any time. I won't ghost you. Even if I'm reading my most favorite book. Haha.

Champa: Aww, that means a lot. You can text or call me whenever you want too.

Rory and Keira

Rory: Did you really lose that photo?

Keira: Yup.

Rory: Why do I not believe you?

Keira: Yes, Rory. Tell me. *Why* do you not believe me?

Rory: Because you wouldn't lose a memory of *us*, right?

Keira: I told you it wasn't deliberate.

Rory: You misplaced just that one photograph?

Keira: Yes.

Rory: It was my favorite one.

Keira: Why? We have other pics of us.

Rory: You know why, Keira.

Keira: Then why do you want me to send it to everyone?

Rory: Share it only with me, then.

Keira: I don't have it.

Rory: Fine, we can just click new pictures the next time we meet. Just the two of us.

Keira: Typing…

~ -- ~

What will happen to Rory and Keira? Will they have a happy ending, or will their relationship fizzle out? Sign up for my newsletter by scanning the QR code below and get a free copy of the five-chapter sequel, "Rory and Keira" delivered to your inbox.

Please Consider Leaving a Review

Thanks for reading. Please leave an honest review on your favorite store for other readers. I would love to read your thoughts too. You can contact me on my website: https://winnzwordz.com.

Other Books by The Author

Published:

Inner Voice Series:

Book 1: Unclutter

Coming Soon:

Sequel to Unclutter

Spin-off of The Mobile Rehab – Champa's and Desmond's story

Scan the QR code below for more information on my books or to follow me on social media.

Acknowledgments

A year ago, I was a debut author, and now I've already published my second book. This has been possible thanks to you all, each and every one of my readers, and your support and encouragement. Thank you for buying my book, loving my stories, and leaving reviews. I love reading your thoughts and comments.

The Mobile Rehab was born five years ago in 2019 when I forgot my phone at home. I was supposed to meet a friend for lunch, but we missed each other. The restaurant chain we'd chosen to dine in had two locations, and each of us went to a different one. I had lunch alone that day, and the concept of this novel formed in my mind.

The same year, my mother talked to me about her travels to Hong Kong, and how she felt it would be almost impossible to survive there without a smart phone. My parents had to stop at many coffee shops that had Wi-Fi for directions and other information. Intrigued, I chose this country for my book.

In November 2019, I participated and completed the NaNoWriMo (National Novel Writing Month) challenge and wrote this book in thirty days. Back then, I hadn't decided whether I was going to publish it.

However, thanks to my mother, I revisited the story last year after releasing my debut novel because it had immense potential. Like her, I, too, felt people would resonate with the concept of smart phone attachment. Thank you again, dear Amma.

After completing my draft, I sent it to my wonderful editor, Shannon Cave, for fine-tuning my manuscript. I didn't *feel* some scenes in the book but was not sure how to fix it. Shannon worked her magic again and guided me to write the story with authenticity and conviction. Thanks again, Shannon.

For the cover, I sent my requirement to the amazing getcovers.com, and their professional designers got my lovely book cover ready within a few days, and I love it. Thank you, getcovers.com.

Since he enjoyed reading my debut novel, my father asked me when the next one was releasing. Most of the time, I didn't have a definite answer, but it motivated me to launch this book on time. So, thank you, dear Annu.

While writing this book, I canceled many movie nights with my husband to "write the next scene that just couldn't wait." Every time, he smiled and encouraged me to finish the novel, so he could read it. Thanks for being so understanding and supportive, my dear.

I mostly burned the midnight oil to write this novel because my days are reserved for my darling daughter. She inspires me to write about subjects and issues she would want to read. I write these stories for you, Baby.

When I got stuck or bored, I could always vent to my fellow author, Naz, who listened patiently without judgment. When I treat my characters like real people, she even plays along. Thanks, Bestie.

I've realized an author must wear multiple hats, out of which the most important one is that of a marketer. I thank my fellow authors and mentors from Author Ad School for the tips to get my work out into the world.

About the Author

Winnie D Pagora loves three things the most in her life: her family, her tech profession, and stories. Her fascination with stories started as a mere toddler when her mother read to her, and she began making up her own when she could barely read or write.

She was just six when her article first got published in a leading children's newspaper in India. Since then, she has written YA contemporary fiction books with strong protagonists, diverse characters, gasp-worthy plot twists, warm 'n' fuzzy friendships, toe-curling romance, and lots of character growth. She published her debut novel, *Unclutter*, in 2023 and her second book, *The Mobile Rehab*, in 2024.

Other than reading and writing, Winnie's interests include travel, wildlife, and global cuisines. She currently lives in Canada with her husband and her daughter.

www.ingramcontent.com/pod-product-compliance
Lightning Source LLC
Chambersburg PA
CBHW051145190726
48290CB00006B/2009